LYON TAMER

JEN LUERSSEN

ISBN: 9798734583951

Publisher: Luerssenperson

Editing: Love Infinity Proofreading

Photo: CJC Photography

Cover Model: Keith Manecke

Cover Design and Formatting: Feed Your Dreams Designs

❀ Created with Vellum

DEDICATION

To the activists, the people who make change happen.

CHAPTER 1

MINIATURE THIRST TRAP

"AM I MISTAKEN, or is that a miniature monster cock?" The low raspy voice startles me and I accidentally shear said monster appendage off.

"Oops," she says with a giggle. "I didn't mean to make you slice that oxymoron free."

My slight irritation disappears when I look up to see the most beautiful woman I've laid eyes on. Her blue-green eyes are smiling, fiery red hair framing her face.

"Hi," she says, waving a hand in front of my face, and I realize I'm just staring like a creeper, holding a tiny severed dick in my hand.

"Uh, hi," I say because I'm cool under pressure. I thought I'd found a secluded little spot in the hotel bar here in Mexico City but I guess not. "This is for my job." What the fuck am I saying?

Her eyes widen in surprise. "Wow, what a job."

She gestures to the empty seat across from me and I must nod because she sits and leans over the vast array of miniatures I'm working on.

When working with miniatures, the most important rule is time equals detail. Meaning, you can't rush something so small if you want it to have a big impact. I've been working in miniature building for years and it helps me with focus and dexterity immensely. Two things that are vital for a veterinarian when performing surgery on a small frog. They may also help when I'm in certain sexy situations. This woman is very thorough in her examination but is respectful enough to not pick any of them up.

"The detail is striking and they look like they are actually fucking. What kind of job requires you to make these?" She points to a couple in the "perch" pose.

I place my tools down and take my magnifying glasses off. I set the polymer mini man and his giant penis down on the wax paper that holds the completed figures I've done since sitting here. Currently, I'm on a 12-hour layover from San Francisco to Guatemala so I've been drinking cranberry juice and sculpting.

"While not sentient beings, they are in a sense, fucking. I could just have them connected where they should be but I like the look of when I make a penis and a vagina opening or mouth and the penetration is legit."

She is staring at me, mouth wide open. I guess that was too much?

"I have so many questions but first, what are you drinking?" she asks pointing to my glass of juice.

After I tell her my order, she gets us each a new drink from the bar and sits. During this time, I've reattached the previously severed appendage and am connecting the figures when she reappears.

"What position would you call that? Looks complicated."

Using tweezers, I slide the female miniature across the male's legs and insert his penis into her vagina. "They are in what's called the 'x-rated' position. The man lies flat on his back and the woman lies on top of him facing away from him with her legs on either side of his waist and her arms wrapped around his legs. She is in the perfect position to slide up and down, while he has an x-rated view of them joining, hence the name."

I realize that maybe I'm being too frank with a stranger when I see the bright red blush across her freckled cheeks. In my family there was far too much frankness about sex, our bodies, etc.—so remembering to have a filter about such things in mixed company is still a challenge. It doesn't help that my friends are all equally open about sex.

"I'm sorry if that was too much information," I say quickly.

"No, it was very graphic, and despite having a physical example, the description helps." She gestures to the finished product and number 77 in my 101 Kama Sutra positions series. "May I ask why you are creating these dirty little minis?"

"In my line of work, precision and attention to detail matters, therefore I create miniatures to keep up my dexterity and focus."

"Why all the sex positions? I'm sure you'd be able to hone your skills just as well if you had them dancing or doing something more benign."

Now it's my turn to blush and I look at the finished products knowing I must look like some perverted deviant. "I like sex, the human form, and have been studying the Kama Sutra for a few years now. The art of making love should be a more popular pursuit, don't you think?"

She laughs heartily. "You think it's not popular enough? I think the multi-billion dollar porn industry may disagree."

"Sure, sex is and always will be popular, but the art of loving someone, body and soul, not just mindless rutting, should be a more universal pursuit."

"Are you implying that a mindless rutting can't be satisfying?" she asks like I've insulted her.

"Not at all," I say, "all sorts of sexual experiences have their place. A quickie in a bathroom, angry makeup sex, fumbling first times when you don't know the person very well. I'm talking about the art of pleasing your partner, bringing them to blissful ecstasy and giving them all of you."

Her cheeks redden again and she licks her lips. "You certainly seem to know what you are doing."

"I guess," I say and look down at the miniatures again. She probably thinks I am some kind of sex addict. She may not be far off base.

Unfortunately, I have no shortage of sexual experiences. I've been with hundreds of women and I thought I was in love with more than half. Now ask me how many relationships have I had—two, that's it. My high school girlfriend, Shelby, I know, Sheldon and Shelby, it was a thing—and Suzy, my last girlfriend before I moved to San Francisco. Suzy and I seem good on paper. We were friends first and I actually waited a week to sleep with her. Usually, I sleep with a woman almost immediately.

Yep.

I'm a serial one-night stander. Not on purpose, although my friend, Frank, says it's self-sabotaging behavior. I see it more as eternal optimism. No one wants a relationship more than me and I always have the best of intentions. The same can't be said for the women I sleep with—for them the connection is physical and temporary. Frank says that because I'm clingy but also objectively good-looking. My other friend Joe says it's my King Kong dick, they want to try it out but find they can't handle it. I don't take any of it personally, but I do find myself alone a lot.

"What is this position called?" she asks, pointing to

a pair where the woman is on her back her legs folded under her, the man slides in beneath her, extending his legs on either side of her head, connected on his lap.

"It's the triumph arch, the man is able to see their connection and attend to her breasts while achieving a deep angle and control of her hips to deep his thrust," I explain, pointing to where he holds her hips.

"Your attention to detail is impressive. Do you use models or just your dirty mind?" she asks looking closely at a couple in the "bridge" pose. "This reminds me of that movie, *Forgetting Sarah Marshall*."

"Ah, yes, probably the only time it's been attempted," I joke, but it's a really hard pose.

She laughs with me and I notice she's blushing again. "I'm not usually this forward with someone I've just met but you leave yourself open with all of these miniatures copulating."

"No need to feel embarrassed, I should probably be the one that feels embarrassment but unfortunately, my hippie parents didn't allow it. No subject was off the table in my house growing up and trust and openness was not only expected but demanded."

"Wow, so you basically are missing the shame gene?"

"Not quite," I say. "There are certainly situations where I'd feel some shame, none that are sexual in nature, obviously."

"So if you were caught doing the bridge pose with

some limber lady by your fellow miniature makers, you'd be cool with it?"

"I've only attempted it once and it was in a locked yoga studio," I say tapping my finger to my lips. "I think that I'd feel pride that I could hold the pose as long as I did without collapsing and hope that my fellow yogis would be impressed."

"Kudos to your sexual prowess. You are okay with public sex then?"

"I wouldn't say I'm okay with it, in that it turns me on but I wouldn't feel shame about someone seeing me finding pleasure with a woman. The thrill of being caught isn't one of my kinks, because I'm not afraid of it I guess." I shrug and think about the last time I did get caught and how uneventful it was. I was penetrating a woman against the wall of our outdoor shower when Frank opened the door, saw us, shrugged and grabbed his wetsuit that had been hanging on a hook next to the lovely woman's head. I never saw her again.

"You are a fascinating person," she says, draining her drink and standing.

"Thanks, I think," I respond, standing with her. "I wish I could say the same about you, but since you've told me almost nothing about yourself, I'll label you a mysterious person."

Her smile is wide and only accentuates her beauty. I lean in and kiss her lightly on the lips.

"I thoroughly enjoyed meeting you, mystery woman."

Normally, this is when I'd invite her to my room, but I have to get up at an ungodly hour and I can't miss my flight. She seems like the type of woman that would make me miss my flight. She pauses, perhaps expecting me to make an offer, but then taps the table and walks out.

I take my phone out and text Suzy.

Me: *I just spent an hour chatting with a beautiful woman and didn't ask her to my room.*
Suzy: *I'm so proud, Shel, but it is fucking three in the morning.*
Me: *Shouldn't you be asleep then?*
Suzy: *You'd think but my ex is doing whatever the opposite of sexting is and here I am.*
Me: *I'm not good at sexting.*
Suzy: *You are not, fortunately for you, you are good at the real sex.*
Me: *Sorry I woke you.*
Suzy: *You're nervous for your trip, I understand.*

I don't get nervous normally, but she isn't totally wrong, I'm excited for this adventure I'm about to go on, and feel some anticipation about what's to come.

Me: *Not nervous.*

Suzy: *Let me guess, you're making miniature porn at the hotel bar, drinking cranberry juice like some weirdo.*

Me: *Looks around the room for cameras.*

Suzy: *It's okay to be nervous about the important trip you are about to embark on. I can't wait to hear about it. You better post updates and pictures.*

Me: *I will. I am aware that it's a once in a lifetime opportunity.*

Suzy: *Okay, go to bed, leave me alone. I am proud of you for not sleeping with the random woman.*

Me: *She wasn't random. I'm proud too, my dick feels less happy about it.*

Suzy: *TMI, bro. Text me when you get to your destination!*

Me: *I will. Thx Suze.*

I put my phone away, carefully put my work in the small toolbox I carry everywhere, and head to my room. I fall asleep imagining my new fiery-haired friend in some of my favorite poses.

CHAPTER 2

LYON'S ROAR

MY UNDERARMS ARE wet with perspiration in the stifling cab. I sip some water from a bottle I purchased at the airport. The introductory email from someone named Simone Lyon includes some tips about traveling in Guatemala. In addition to advice on what types of clothes to bring and to not drink the tap water, suggestions were made to exchange money at the airport, pack a mosquito net and a jacket as it may get a bit chilly at night. January in Guatemala has warm days and cool nights.

Another thing she mentioned was that people drive like maniacs here and there aren't many rules on the road. Also, a trip that is billed as taking an hour may in reality be closer to two hours. My eyes have been closed most of the trip to the encampment not far from Guatemala City where I'm going to be staying for the next week. My taxi driver seems to be from the 'fuck it' school of driving so I've put my mind on the same setting. He speeds through the city to the bumpy roads on the outskirts—in this case the email was incorrect, my driver got us here in under 30 minutes when I was told the encampment was about an hour away. As we pull into a long dirt driveway, I notice the temporary sign with the Freedom Roar Rescue Org. logo on it.

I'm here to replace a vet who had a family emergency and had to bow out. My mission is to care for about a dozen lions and tigers, rescued from local circuses and zoos in Guatemala. They are being relocated to a reserve in South Africa, where they will live out their lives in peace, far away from the abuse and neglect of their former homes. Because of over breeding and malnourishment, some of the cats have birth defects, seizures, and all have suffered brutal declawing, tooth removal and were kept in heartbreaking conditions.

The car stops in front of a large tent that looks like it's been there for a while but very sturdy. The driver removes my duffle from the trunk and stands with his hand out. I give him about 100 quetzals (about $13 US) which is probably too much but he did get me here quickly despite fearing for my life most of the way.

I load my backpack and duffel over my shoulder and head inside the tent. The tent is stifling and empty of people. It's set up as an office or a command center and

I can see laptops, a printer, and paper everywhere. There's camera equipment as well for filming. I drop my two bags behind one of the tables and head back outside bumping into a small person.

"Oof!" I lean down to help the person up and I immediately get even sweatier. The woman currently dusting herself off after a much larger man knocked her down is none other than the red-headed beauty I met last night. She hasn't noticed me yet since she's picking pebbles from her thigh. A very shapely thigh, smooth and pale, a light dusting of freckles matching the rest of her, I imagine—then I start imagining things I should not.

"Mystery woman," I say flatly, not knowing how this encounter is going to proceed. Her first impressions of me are sketchy at best. A man creating miniatures in compromising positions and now a brute who is clearly not watching where he is going. My hands quickly go from her shoulders to my side after helping her upright but she may still be angry I touched her without permission. I'm sure I'm worrying for nothing but my luck is bad in all aspects of my life except my career and I'd like to keep that one part of my life worry free. "Are you okay? I apologize for my lack of body awareness."

Her eyes shoot up at me and I'm expecting some wrath. She does a full up and down assessment of me and when she sees my face her smile puts me instantly at ease. "It's you," she says. "The mini-perv."

"Uh, yes, that's I, although I don't find my interest in the art of Kama Sutra to be a perversion, but an attempt at self-improvement." This is going well.

She laughs and holds her hand out. "I'm Simone Lyon, and I assume you are our veterinarian?"

I take her hand and it's surprisingly cool and soft. "Yes, Sheldon Locke, but you can call me Shel."

"Well, Shel, welcome to Cat Camp." Her arms spread wide like she's about to give me a tour of *Jurassic Park*. "Can I show you around?"

"Sure, should I retrieve my bags from the tent?" I say pointing my thumb behind me.

"Yes, grab them and I'll show you to your bunk so you can drop them there."

Once I have them, I follow her brisk pace around the main tent to a small courtyard where several other smaller tents are located in a circle.

"These are our quarters, two people to a tent." She twirls her finger around and then points to one. "Lucky you, you will share with me," she adds sounding not super excited about it.

I follow her into the tent, through a double mosquito net inside the door. Once inside I see it's not as small as I thought. There are two twin-size cot beds with a large table in between. A trunk sits at the bottom of each bed and one has small boots sitting on top of a canopy mosquito net draped over the bed.

"This is your cot, hopefully you've brought the net

we recommended. Even with the double net at the door, the pests can get through. We've inspected both cots for bed bugs and they are free, so you should be able to sleep without much discomfort."

I place my bags on the empty trunk and open my backpack to take out the exact net she has on her cot. I shake it a few times and then suspend it from a hook kindly provided above my new resting place for the next week.

"Make sure to put your things in the trunk, keeps everything dry and free of scorpions," she laughs at my expression of terror. "Just kidding, they are generally harmless but tend to stay out of your way. You have a likelier chance of a tiger bite in this camp."

After my things are put away, we head back out and she takes me on a path past the tents and the distinct smell of animal hits me. Ahead, I see the large caged in areas where the cats are kept and I hear a roar, it's unlike any other sound and I love it. The few years I spent at the San Francisco Zoo will help me navigate this adventure as well as the copious reading I did at home and on the plane.

"Tiger?" I ask knowing it probably is. A tiger's roar sounds more like what we expect a lion to sound like. In fact, they used tiger roars in the *Lion King*.

"Yes, that would be Quique, our most vocal and ornery tiger. He is also the largest and wildest of the bunch." I follow her as she walks toward the source of the roar.

"Keekay, is that Spanish?" I ask.

"Yes, it's a nickname for Enrique and means ruler of the house. Quique for sure thinks he is in charge."

"He sounds formidable." Most big cats tend to be, but after years of living in captivity, most are tame and docile.

"That he is, but mostly he's all bark and no bite. Especially because his teeth were filed down and his claws were removed with pliers." She shakes her head. "That's not to say he's not still dangerous—he is the biggest cat we have here but he's been tortured for years."

"I'm sure he just loves humans then," I half laugh because it's not funny what they did to him. "Luckily for him, his human interactions will be limited once he's in Africa."

She comes to a padlocked gate and unlocks it. Razor wire lines the top of a high wire fence. We both pass in and she re-locks it. "It's very important that we keep this locked at all times. If someone really wanted to steal these guys, they can get through but it will slow them down. It's more for their protection so no one messes with the cats. I'll get you a key later."

I nod and take in the amazing view before me. There are about a dozen large cages spaced out, some with families of cats, some with just one or two, a few are empty. Instantly, I find Keekay as he is letting me know how unwelcome I am. I approach his cage and see in large writing that his name is spelled Q-u-i-q-u-e. On one side of him is a pair of what look to be young adults, named Venus and Mars.

"Venus and Mars are a little under a year old and are siblings. On this side of Quique, is Jax, Jada, Miguel and Lana—all of his kids, along with Gala and Fabia, his wives." As large and imposing as Quique is, his family are on the small side. "Fabia is one that we watch pretty closely because of seizures."

She introduces me to Tasha and Kamal a sweet pair of tigers, they both come to the front of their cage and chuff at me—a tiger's way of saying hello. Next, we cross to the corner where there are two lions in one cage.

"This is Gloria and Emilio, they are very attached to one another. Gloria fought another tiger that was attacking poor Emilio. You'll see he has an injury on his muzzle. We are hoping you can stitch him up a bit better before the trip."

Gloria is stretched across the ground with Emilio safely tucked behind her, she eyes me warily.

"Hola, bellezas," I say clearly. The email specifically asked me to bone up on a few nice Spanish phrases to say to the animals. These two are beauties for sure and a sense of purpose washes over me. This is important work the organization is doing. Wild animals should not be used for human entertainment. The conditions these animals tolerated are ghastly and I'm proud to be a part of moving them to a better place, a better life.

"Come with me, Shel, I'll show you where you can wash up and then the most important place here—the cantina." She makes jazz hands and I laugh.

I'm overwhelmed and exhausted but ready to work. I follow Simone to the bathroom which is a row of sinks outside and some solar warmed showers like you'd see in an old school army camp with wooden planks covering only the mid-part of your body. The latrine is located across from the showers and are basically port-o-potties. I use the latrine and the sink to wash my hands and face then meet her at our tent.

"The cot looks pretty inviting, I know, I've only been here a few hours and I'm already dead on my feet." she teases when she sees me eye it longingly. "Let's get you some food, we can chat and then you can have a nap." She pats my shoulder. "Let's go Mini-perv."

"Hey, I'm here to do a job, can we let go of the nick-name?" I hope that didn't sound harsh.

She laughs, a beautiful, loud cackle. "Sure thing, *Doctor* Mini-perv."

CHAPTER 3

MEET AND GREET

THE SOUNDS of the camp are loud and strange. Roars from the cats are sporadic, roosters cackle, and insects create a symphony. It's so dark I can barely make out the netting draped around me. Last but not least is the woman in the bunk not far from mine. Her breaths are long and deep, punctuated by the occasional Disney princess-like sigh. If I fall asleep tonight, it will be a miracle.

Exhaustion sunk into my bones not long after I met all of the cats and a few of the workers. I also briefly met the founders of the rescue, Nancy and Nigel. The couple seemed grateful to see me and were in constant motion, either on their phones, walkie-talkies or fielding questions from one of the other workers. They handed me a folder with an overview of every animal under their care.

Simone then led me to the cantina and put a full plate of rice and beans and grilled plantains in front of me. I ate quickly and then sat at a desk she had shown me earlier in the main tent, to read over the cat files. They all seem to be in relatively good health but some have issues. Three of the tigers have seizure disorders and two have severe diarrhea. Some have birth defects from inbreeding and the mother's malnourishment. All are headed to a better life and I'm honored to be a part of it.

One of the local workers shook me awake, my head resting on the open file. Luckily, I didn't drool on anything important and headed to my bunk. I've been here ever since, unable to rest my mind, block out the unfamiliar noise, and unable to not think of her, next to me.

Since I arrived, she's mostly ignored me unless it was to show me where to eat or work. She didn't sit and join me at dinner, nor did she linger after showing me to my desk. Maybe I'm reading more into our first meeting, which is very much on-brand for me, so Suzy tells me.

My mind wanders to the kiss we shared. It wasn't one of those deep soul-baring kisses, but more of a sweet promise. Her soft lips returned the small pressure of mine as she kissed me back. I can't say for certain, but if I had asked her, I think she would have come to my room. My regret and relief at not doing that are equal. If we had a dalliance, it would have made working here even more awkward than it is. The sweetness of her lips and the heat in her eyes may have made it all worth it. Not a trace of that heat was to be found today in my interactions with her.

A sigh comes from her bunk and it's decidedly not a sigh a princess from a children's movie would make. More like a sigh elicited from a lover's soft caress. In the darkness, I can't see her face, but I imagine her lips parted, cheeks flushed over those freckles, her hand lightly drifting over her breast. Yeah, sleep isn't happening for me anytime soon.

I must have fallen asleep eventually because I wake to Simone cursing under her breath. In the low light of our lantern, I can see her bent at the waist over her trunk, most of her hidden. The top closes and I see her now, in a sleeveless nightgown hitting her very high on her thighs. She sets a pile of clothes on the trunk and turns to look at my side of the tent. I keep my eyes closed, feigning sleep. After a few seconds, I open them a sliver to watch her as she quickly gets dressed. I barely see anything as she pulls her pants on under her gown and then turns her back to me to take it off.

Creamy freckled skin with considerable muscle tone meets my eyes and I'm unable to look away as she pulls a sports bra over her head and then a tank top. I watch, mesmerized as she applies sunscreen to every place her skin is exposed. It must feel like a part-time job keeping herself from being burned from the sun. I'm sure she must reapply every hour. She then collects her long copper hair and ties it in a ponytail, then creates some elaborate braid that looks impossible.

"Dr. Mini-perv, you need a camera?" Oops.

I meet her eyes and she doesn't look angry but slightly annoyed. "A camera?" I ask like the dolt I clearly am.

"I believe the kids say—take a picture it'll last longer," she says, sarcasm dripping from her words. "It's time to get up."

That's all she says as she puts on a fleece over her tank top and leaves me in silence. I want to feel bad, but I don't. If she didn't want me to see her change, she would have gone to the latrine. Simone doesn't strike me as someone who is ashamed of her body or is particularly modest. I spent my childhood around people with zero hang-ups and not a lot of clothing. Many of my childhood photos are of my bare bottom or my penis swinging in the breeze. My mom laughs and says I was allergic to pants until I was about eight if you ask her about it.

I stretch my long limbs and crack my neck before I get up and then go through a series of yoga poses I do daily. My body has been folded into small beds, even smaller plane seats and the cot I'm sleeping in for the next few weeks with my feet hanging over the edge. My size has advantages, but it can feel like a burden, especially when trying to fit into a space made for an average-sized human. I'm hanging upside down in a forward fold when I hear the zipper on the tent door.

"Good God, I thought you'd be dressed by now," Simone squeaks out.

I rise and turn to her. Her eyes do a quick dip to my boxer brief covered crotch, and I smile. My morning erection has subsided while practicing yoga but I am a shower and a grower, or Suzy tells me. Simone turns away and I chuckle.

After I am dressed in shorts and a hoodie, the morning is a little brisk but the heat is there, waiting for later, Simone and I head to the cantina. We eat in silence, oatmeal and coffee, warming me. It's ridiculously early but the schedule I received from Simone yesterday listed wake up at 5 am and here we are.

"Not a morning person Dr. Mini-perv?" she asks as I fill my coffee cup for the third time.

I smile at her using my nickname. "Not really, but I don't mind being up early. Just takes three cups of coffee to get my mind to catch up to my body."

She blushes and I smile again, she's thinking about my body. I know it's a good-looking body, as I've been told by many. It doesn't matter to me what it looks like, but I like it to perform well. Suzy teases me about my slab of abs and python arms—her words—when she's not telling every woman she meets about my legendary penis. Thankfully, I've known her long enough that I know she appreciates my mind and heart equally. I know how I affect women. I just don't always know how to react to their attention.

"How do you maintain all of that?" Simone interrupts my wandering thoughts. "It must take half of your day lifting weights just to keep those abs in six-pack form."

Simone's arms are crossed as she looks at me with curiosity. She's in pretty great shape herself and I wonder what she does for exercise.

"I have a schedule of things I do, but I'm in maintenance mode and can keep my abs in form by practicing yoga, doing core work, and light cardio. It helps to have spent my childhood farming. It's not all work, some of it is the luck of the DNA draw." Her face is blank and then she smiles.

"Okay, well Dr. DNA, let's get started on these cats."

"I feel like Dr. DNA might sound different to some ears. Can we just go with Shel or at least Dr. Locke?" I ask, maybe begging a little.

She looks like she's about to call me something worse when Nancy and Nigel walk in.

"Dr. Mini-perv, Ms. Lyon," Nigel says in a loud and

boisterous voice, way too loud and boisterous for the early hour.

I shoot Simone a look because he said my name like it was my actual name. Like he thinks Mini-perv is truly my name. Do I correct him and look foolish or let him call me Dr. Mini-perv for all eternity? Again, not a decision for this early in the day, so I choose to go with the flow.

"Good morning, Nigel and Nancy," I say in a quiet, morning appropriate level.

"Morning Nance and Nige," Simone says casually. "He actually prefers Shel, dontcha Dr. Mini-perv."

I hide my face in my hands because I need a fourth cup of coffee and maybe a five-mile run.

"Shel it is then, old boy!" Nigel says in an exaggerated British accent. He and Nancy are from London just don't speak with as hard of an accent as he is currently putting out there. "Better eat your gruel and drink your cuppa and get to taming them big kittens."

Simone and Nancy are cracking up and I smile at all of them, probably looking a bit crazed. Nigel pats me on the back.

"We're fucking with you boy," he says in a normal tone he used when I first met him. "Simone here told us you dabble in miniature making, is that so?"

My eyes dart toward Simone and she winks at me. "I told them about our first encounter, you didn't seem to be the type to be bashful about your hobby."

"I do like to craft miniatures, it helps with hand dexterity, and concentration. If I'm patient enough to craft a miniature version of a Pomeranian then I'll have the patience to operate on a real-sized version."

"Fascinating," Nancy comments and then claps her hands. "You'll have to make miniature of all our pussies."

Simone pulls both of her lips in to keep from laughing and I just stare longingly at the coffee maker, willing it to just hook up to my central nervous system.

Nigel claps along with Nancy as they start chanting 'mini pussies' and I'm not sure if I'm really awake or still dreaming. The three of them start laughing again and I know they are still messing with me.

"Welcome to Freedom Roar Camp, Shel," Simone says with a twinkle in her eye.

CHAPTER 4

HERE KITTY KITTY

TIGER POOP IS pungent generally but tiger diarrhea is a whole other level. Weirdly, tiger urine smells like buttered popcorn—unfortunately there's copious amounts of it. Two of the tigers, Kamal and Tasha have a severe case of diarrhea and are being treated. Sadly for us, the treatment takes a while. Their cage is located in a corner set back a little so when they do their business it doesn't soil the other cats or their cages. Staying safely out of the line of fire is a challenge, but I'm in heaven just being here with these magnificent animals.

After we finish breakfast, Nancy walks through the cat area with me and we go through a chart for each one. I help Diego and Sal, two of the local hires with feeding and I administer medications and tend to Emilio's lip wound. Most of the cats are docile but little risk is taken here I've found. Most medication is given orally, but a few need to be injected or applied to a wound. Either the cat is sedated or restrained, which I can tell they don't like to do, but it's a necessity to keep everyone safe.

After a lunch of peanut soup, I sit alone in the cantina looking over some notes about Emilio and the minor surgery his lip requires when Simone bursts through the door.

"Dr. DNA! All hands on deck, there's a rescue in the works." I haven't seen her since this morning's hazing and she looks stunning. Her hair is loose around her face as hair escapes from her braid, she's flush with excitement, her eyes are shining, and her bare arms are covered in a light sheen of sweat. I'm just about to answer her when she heads back out the door she came in.

I follow her to the main tent where Rico-leader of camp operations, Nancy, Nigel, and Diego are bent over a sprawling unfolded map.

"Shel, good, you're here," Nigel says in a much more serious tone than this morning. The camp, I've found, is very serious when it comes to the care and rescue of the cats, everything else is game for making fun. "We've tracked down a lion here," he says pointing to a place on the map. "We are doing some planning and hope to rescue her tomorrow morning."

The Guatemalan government has recently outlawed using wildlife in circuses but has been spotty on enforcement. The Freedom Roar rescue takes on these small circuses and rescues the tigers and lions with the help of local law enforcement. This was all explained to me when I spoke with Nancy on the phone when she asked me to come. My mistake was assuming they'd collected all the animals they could and were ready to move them next week.

"Okay, what can I do to help? Get a cage ready?" I ask.

Simone grabs my wrists. "Oh no, Dr. Mini-perv," she says and we're back to that I guess? "You and I are going on a mission."

The look of horror on my face must show because everyone in the room laughs.

"Oh, Shel, don't look so worried, my guy." Rico places his hand on my shoulder. "We'll make sure you have a rifle and a whole lot of quetzals to bargain with."

Nigel waves his hand. "Don't scare him, Rico, there won't be need for a gun. The circus has been moving a lot because they know we are looking for lions to rescue. They probably think we will either give up or won't find them and maybe the new government will rescind the law."

"What?" I ask.

"Well, like I told you, we are on a time crunch here. The government turns over in about three weeks and there's a chance they'd change the law back or not be as friendly about enforcing the law. This is why we need to get these cats out quickly," Nancy explains. "We got lucky, one of Rico's cousins lives in the town where the circus showed up and now, we know where they are."

"Transport leaves at 6 am. Simone and Sheldon will be on the flatbed and Nigel and I the pickup. Nancy will stay here with Diego and Sal to care for the cats and keep the camp safe." I stare at Rico in a daze, like this is some movie or something. Me, on a rescue mission? I'm thrilled and terrified.

We continue to go over strategy, negotiating tactics, and signs that things may get violent. They weren't joking about us having a rifle but reassured me that they'd never had to use one before.

"This is my third round of rescue and transport with Freedom Roar and promise it will work out," Simone says reassuring me. "Come on, let's help with watering the cats, eat dinner and turn in early."

We help Sal fill all the water bowls and spray some lavender oil around the tiger cages because they love the smell and it does help cover some of the aforementioned poop odor. We eat a delicious dinner of a thick stew called pepián—made with beans to keep it vegan, by a young local man named Beto. He makes all the food for the camp and brings in the meat for the cats. I know, the humans are vegan but the cats are not. He speaks no English but is the friendliest person in the cantina. I struggle through some basic Spanish, complimenting him on his cooking. He seems to be happy with me, smiling and shaking my hand.

After dinner, I take a quick shower and then take Simone's suggestion and get into my cot. She follows shortly after and we lay in silence for a bit. As exhausted as I am, I know I'm going to struggle to fall asleep.

"Are you nervous?" she asks.

"A little, more of just the unknown of it all." My mind is racing with all that can go wrong. "Probably the most nervous about driving the flatbed truck with a lion cage on it—with actual lions inside."

She laughs. "No worries, I'll drive it. You should be more concerned with roving gangs and getting lost. Not to mention the roads are not well maintained and we could easily get a flat or even break an axle. Stuck in the Guatemalan wilderness forever."

"Why do you insist on giving me a hard time?" I ask. "I thought I made an impression on you the night we met."

Her sigh is loud and long. "You're right, you did. Since you've shown up, I've been so thrown for a loop I've been using my cheeky defense mechanism. That's on me and I apologize. Nancy and Nigel are very impressed by you, don't let their casual attitudes fool you."

"I think I'm understanding the dynamic here at camp more each day. It's serious business but it's also inspiring and joyful. The levity is necessary." I swat a rogue mosquito that has gotten through my netting and turn to face her bunk. I can just see her face in the low light of the lantern I left on so she could see when she came back. "I feel like we should talk about the moment we had at the hotel."

"It was a good moment, and one I thought was fleeting so it felt even more special. Then you're here the next day and the moment is just a memory now." She props herself up on her elbow to look at me. "I like you, doctor, and I'm happy you've joined us, but we have work to do and I need us to concentrate on that—despite what moments have come before."

I nod in agreement. "I'm good with that, but don't feel like you have to be weird around me, I like you too and respect all that you've done with Freedom Roar. How did you end up in this job?"

She flops down on her cot and laughs. "How did I end up with those two nutters?" she asks rhetorically. "Nigel and my dad were best friends growing up and were in a band together. When I graduated, I had a communications degree and was looking to work in PR for a non-profit. I'd visited the rescue site in Colorado a few times and when Nigel heard I was looking he hired me on the spot. Pure nepotism is why I'm here. Why are you here?"

"I guess nepotism as well? When your vet had to leave, he contacted my partner and asked if she would replace him and she couldn't take the time away from her kids so she recommended me. I'm single and have no life other than work so I was the perfect fit. Plus, I have a rehab license and good experience with large mammals."

She laughs. "Being a large mammal yourself."

"Yes, I'm an above average sized male human. You are pretty tall for a female human."

"I guess at 5' 10" I'm tall for a female human. You've got at least a hundred pounds of muscle on me though."

"Perhaps, you seem very fit though, do you run?"

"Only from scorpions and snakes. I do some yoga and was a pretty serious dancer until I broke my ankle in college. I still dance, but my pipe dream of doing it professionally is long gone." She looks sad for a minute but then shakes it off.

"Where did you grow up?" I ask.

"In Berkeley, my dad moved there from London when he was very young and was in a punk band. He runs a music label and is pretty successful. My mom owns a pre-school and they still live in the house I grew up in. When I went to school in Rhode Island, they lost their minds."

"Brown?" I ask and she nods. "Fancy Ivy League school. I'm impressed."

She shrugs. "I got a full ride for dance so I couldn't say no. How about you, doctor? What place made you?"

"New Jersey, naturally—it's a scientific fact that the most interesting people come from Jersey," I say and she laughs. She has a great laugh. "My parents are still there in the house I grew up in too. It's more of a farm, but I can't imagine them ever leaving it, even after they die. I'm sure they want to be buried in the soil to nourish the life they leave behind."

Again, she laughs. "They sound interesting."

"My parents are old school hippies and are proud of it. They sell organic veggies and goat cheese to local restaurants and probably are some of the originators of farm-to-table before it was called that. I had a very free upbringing, which is why I'm more rigid in my adulthood, so my mother tells me."

My parents let me free range raise myself from an early age. This led to a few trust issues and a need for affection that I've not yet slaked. It also led me to my life's calling. Since I was left to my own devices, I found the only friends I could within miles of our farm, animals. My best friend was a pygmy goat, Missy, until I was five and she was violently killed by a coyote. I tried to save her but she had lost too much blood.

"Wow, I can totally see you as a farm boy. It all makes sense, you've looked like this since you were a teen, huh?"

"I suppose, farm work definitely is a workout and I love getting my hands dirty when I go visit my parents."

"Making those miniatures redefines getting your hands dirty." We both laugh and I feel better about us working together in the coming weeks. "How did you get into that? Don't say *hand dexterity*," she says mocking my deep voice.

"In vet school one of the things I struggled with was working with smaller animals since I have what my mother calls catcher's mitt hands." I lift my hands and wiggle them. "One of my professors advised me to take up a hobby to help with being more precise. After consulting Google, miniature making was the first thing that came up. I started with animals and have evolved into food, then humans, and more recently the Kama Sutra. When he noticed my improvement, I told him why and he looked surprised. He meant for me to start knitting or doing hand exercises, I guess. It's fun and when I finish a series, I donate most of them to my local library."

"You are very good, I'm sure it could be a profitable side gig."

"I don't have time for another job, but I have done some commissioned pieces but I don't charge."

"I'm curious who would commission such a thing?"

"You'd be surprised. I've done a series of cats for one of my clients, some mini food for a local restaurant, and one man wanted a series of his wife doing everyday things." I like being creative on my own, and it's another way to exercise my mind, but doing commissions are fun too.

"Hmm, not as creepy as I thought." She yawns and then so do I.

"I think it's because you encountered me making miniatures of a sexual nature, so that would lead you to believe that's all I do."

"Yeah, that was a pretty odd sight to see at a hotel bar."

"I was shocked you sat with me, usually the miniatures work as a deterrent to other people."

"I guess I'm drawn to the depraved."

"Sexuality and loving a sexual partner in a healthy way isn't depraved," I say.

"Of course it isn't, some would say making miniature representations of sexual acts *is*."

"True, I can see that my art could be misconstrued as such."

She laughs again and I can't get enough of it. "Okay, my artist friend, we should really try to sleep. Tomorrow is going to be a long day."

"Thank you," I say quietly.

"For what?" she asks.

"For calling me your friend." My voice is barely a whisper and her smile makes me feel warm.

She leans over and turns the lantern off. "Goodnight, Dr. Mini-perv."

CHAPTER 5

MISSION IMPOSSIBLE

OF ALL THE things I thought might go wrong this morning, me having violent car sickness was at the bottom of the list. Simone and I are heading to a small town north of Guatemala City and the road to get there is bumpy. We were fine for about an hour out of the city but then the road started to wind a little and the ruts and divots started my stomach roiling.

Currently, I'm hanging out the passenger window losing my breakfast, last night's dinner and pretty much anything I've eaten in recent memory. Simone has not slowed down the flatbed truck as time is of the essence. If the circus gets wind of us coming, they will just bail or hide the animals before we arrive.

"I'm so sorry, Shel," she says patting my back.

I take a large gulp of fresh air and try to pull myself together as I sit back in my seat. "Please don't be nice right now," I say in a raspy whisper. "For some reason, I need you to make fun of me and be a little mean about it."

"Oh no, Dr. DNA, are you one of those whiny little men who need a lady to be a bitch to get you off?" she taunts me. "I thought someone as big and strong as you would have an iron stomach."

I wipe the sweat from my brow with the bottom of my shirt, giving her a slight nod of approval. She hands me a bottle of water from the cooler nestled in between us. I rest its coolness on my face and then take a few sips. I find a stick of gum in my pocket and pop it in my mouth, it helps a little.

"Thanks," I say glancing at her profile. She's stunning in her polo shirt, khaki shorts and her hair in two braids that spool down past her shoulders. Her face is fixed in concentration as she navigates the terrain. She shrugs. "I can't even explain why kindness when I'm ill makes me feel worse."

"Ha! Yeah, the drive isn't long enough to unpack that particular neurosis."

I lay my head back and close my eyes. "Let me know when we are almost there."

I don't hear what she says as I slowly descend into a restorative nap, but it sounds vaguely like 'useless.'

What feels like only a few minutes later, our walkie-talkie beeps loudly. They are necessary where cell reception is spotty and that is about 80% of the country.

I roll my head and am able to lift the small plastic communication device so I can turn up the volume.

"Come in Pennywise, this is Candyman…come in Pennywise." Nigel's voice squeaks over the walkie. I look at Simone and she is smiling.

"Nancy adores horror movies and books. We thought code names would make it seem more like a *Mission Impossible* movie." She shifts down and we pull over.

"Pennywise here, go ahead Candyman, over," Simone replies after taking it from me.

"Just confirming your location, what's your ETA? Over."

"We are about 5 miles from target with a 15 minute ETA, over." I start to sweat and not from feeling ill or the heat in the truck, which has no air conditioning. I'm nervous and I feel like a sheltered loser.

"10-4, we are turning back, there's a problem at camp, confirm you are on mission, over."

"Shit," Simone says and now I'm drenched in flop sweat.

"10-4, we are on mission, will make contact when we are coming back to base, over."

"Godspeed, Pennywise. You and Krueger should be a go for rescue," he says and the walkie-talkie screeches and goes silent.

"Shit, shit, shit," Simone chants and I'm not the only nervous one.

"Does he call you Pennywise because of your hair?" I ask.

She looks at me like I'm the nuisance I am. "Really? That's your question? Not I wonder what's going on at camp, or maybe why are you saying shit over and over?"

"Well, I can see you are freaking out, he didn't tell us what's happening so there's not much we can do about it, and I'm trying to distract us both with a dumb question."

"Yes, he thinks it's the funniest thing he's ever thought of, and Nancy calls him Wonka because he makes all her dreams come true so that's the Candyman connection. You are Freddy Krueger because you're the vet and use a scalpel. Ha ha, all hilarious, but what do we do now? I've never done a rescue on my own."

"You're not on your own, you have me," I say and she looks even more panicked. "Okay, so I don't have any experience and I don't speak Spanish, but I'm big and I can look scary." I make what I think is a scary face.

She looks horrified. "Oh my God, do *not* make that face. How are you a giant but you look like a sweet teddy bear? We're going to die."

"Let's do some breathing," I say. "Four counts in and then four counts out."

She looks skeptical but when I start counting, she does the breathing with me. After a few rounds of breath, we are both calm and she resumes driving to our destination. We arrive at the circus camp and people immediately scatter.

"Let me do the talking," she says. "Usually, we have Rico to do it but he got in the wrong truck today."

I shrug. "I'll follow your lead. Remember the mission and all will be well."

All was not well.

Simone pulls the flat bed close to where we think the lions are housed. When we get out, there's not a person to be seen. The telltale scent of animal is pungent and I can see movement in one of the crates nearby. We walk together towards the animal crates and we both still when we see the lions. There are two and we were only expecting one. It looks like a mother and an older cub.

Simone gasps next to me. "It's Lala," she whispers. I'm not sure who Lala is but Simone is very happy to see her. She approaches the small cage and coos. "Bonita, Lala, hola, Lala."

She says a series of things in Spanish and I only catch a few things about her being a mom, pretty, that she's sorry they couldn't save her sooner. Lala sits like a quiet sphinx occasionally blinking or swishing her tail. I can see she's filthy and a bit malnourished, much like the other cats we have in our camp. Her cub is cleaner, probably because she tends to him, but also looks malnourished and a little lethargic.

"We need to get them out of here," Simone says and I agree but while she's been cooing at Lala, two women have approached and one has a rifle slung around her arm. Not pointed at us but it's a presence. I gently nudge Simone and she stands and faces the women.

She asks them a question in Spanish and they reply calmly. Simone seems to relax a little until she asks them another and they start shouting at her.

"What's going on?" I ask.

"I told them I'm here to help the lions and they were happy until I told them we were taking them." One of the women steps closer, trying to shoo us away from the cage. Like we'd be able to pick up a 400-pound lion and her cub and just skip away. We need to get them to agree and then help us load them onto our truck.

Simone continues her discussion with the women and shows them the order to surrender the lions, mentioning the police. The women turn and walk away.

"They are considering my offer and will return with a counter most likely. They know they have to give them up but they are a big money maker for them so they want some compensation. I'm willing to go higher than they expect." The women are now arguing loudly and gesturing to me.

"I thought Rico's cousin was supposed to meet us

here?" I ask. He would have made things go more smoothly I'd imagine.

Simone shrugs. "He was, but I don't have his number and Rico would need to be in range to call him to meet us. He'll be here to help us load the lions hopefully."

"What's taking so long? Are they stalling?"

"Nah, they are making us sweat or they're going to try to get us to let them keep one, probably Lala." She looks at her watch and mops her brow with the underside of her shirt. I catch a flash of her abdomen and all the creamy skin there. Focus, Shel, not the time.

"Maybe they're waiting for the men to show up?" I ask.

She laughs. "We should be so lucky. The men would be easy, hand them cash and we'd already be on the road. The women are shrewder and know the worth of the animals, despite the law and may be willing to risk keeping them. We should be more scared of them than any man." She waves her hand at me in dismissal.

I nod and stand corrected. The women finally finish their discussion and walk to us. The younger of the two speaks to us in clear English.

"We want to keep the cub, and two thousand for the mother." She stands firm, arms crossed.

"How about 4,000 for both and I don't call the policia." Simone counters.

"5,000 and we don't make you load them on your own," the woman says with a scowl.

"Deal," Simone says and they shake hands. "Doctor, once we get them on the truck, you'll pay the woman," she says, hitting me on the chest with the back of her hand.

We get the truck back up and closer to the lions and then roll the cage we brought down the truck's ramp. About the time we get the cages lined up, Rico's cousin, Eric, shows up. He brought a friend so we should be able to roll the full cage back up the ramp with their help. I get the rabbit meat from the cooler we brought and lure the two lions into the cage with the meat.

Once the transfer is complete, the older woman shouts and points the rifle at us. All of our hands go up immediately. Eric and his friend start shouting in Spanish at her and they all start yelling.

Simone puts two fingers in her mouth and whistles loudly enough to get everyone's attention in this hemisphere. "Alto!" she shouts and then turns to me. "She wants the money, they are afraid we will stiff them, now that we have more muscle. Pay the lady, Shel."

I walk over to the woman with the rifle still pointed at us and point to my pocket. "Quetzals," I say and she nods, lowering the gun then thrusting her hand into my pocket, taking the entire wad of cash. I hold my hand out so she can give back the extra 2,000 I had in my pocket and she laughs at me, shoving the money down the front of her dress.

When I turn around Simone is glaring at me. I put my arms out and shrug. "It's my first time."

She mumbles a curse and shakes her head, walking to one side of the cage. The four of us each take a corner and then push to roll it up the ramp. It doesn't budge and the older lady laughs. I position myself at the back of the cage and the younger woman from the circus steps in to take my spot. After a few tries, we finally get the cage up the ramp and onto the truck. Simone and Eric secure it to the bed using straps and winches.

About an hour after we've arrived, we finally load ourselves into the truck after thanking Eric and giving him some money as well. I'm buckling myself in when Simone stops me with her arm on mine.

"Wait," she says. Looking to where the lions once were and squinting like she's listening. "Get in the driver's seat and start the truck."

She slides quietly out of the truck and I slip over to the steering wheel and turn the keys, firing up the truck. I lose sight of Simone for a minute and then hear her shouting before I see her.

"Start driving, Shel, go!" I hear her call out and then I see her running to me, her one hand waving wildly for me to go and the other holding a bundle. I have started rolling, headed in the direction of the main road when she swings herself up, places the bundle through the window, then opens the door and hops in, all in about a half a second. "Go, go, go!" she says again and I work the clutch and shift into gear, pulling away.

I'm just pulling on to the road when I hear a loud bang that sounds like a gunshot. I shift into third and speed up, putting more distance between the circus and us. When I look in the rearview, I see the older woman running behind us shooting the rifle in the air. We are too far away for her to get a shot at us, thank goodness.

I turn to Simone and come face to face with a small monkey sitting in her lap. "What is that?" I ask.

"This is a baby howler monkey," she whispers, "and I'm pretty sure she wasn't part of our deal."

CHAPTER 6

ADRENALINE UNICORN

WE ARE both silent as I drive back the way we came. When we get in cell phone range, Simone calls Nancy's phone. Simone relays what happened and our unexpected rescue of the monkey.

"He's just a baby, I couldn't leave him," Simone says in the sweetest baby voice. "Serves her right for taking that extra 2000 quetzals."

I keep my eyes on the road, knowing it's important for us to get closer to a populated area. There are buildings and a few gas stations we pass, but we are still far from the city.

"Okay, we will head there," Simone says, still talking with Nancy, presumably. "I know, but he handled getting shot at like a champ."

I steal a glance at her and she's cuddling with the monkey. I thought she was speaking about me and how well I've not lost my mind over getting shot at but maybe she means the monkey. She chats for a few more minutes and writes a few things down on a small piece of paper, leaning on the dash, while still cradling the little guy. She hangs up and turns to me.

"Okay, we are headed to a new destination, to drop this little cutie off," she says and my adrenaline spikes again. Traveling to new places in the unknown, hopefully this time there will be fewer firearms.

"Just let me know when to turn," I respond, not wavering in my concentration on the road.

After about 30 minutes, we reach a farm or a ranch, not exactly sure what it is. Simone directs me to the side of a large white building that looks somewhat like a barn. She's spent the entire ride sweet-talking the monkey and ignoring me.

I stay in the truck while she hands the monkey over to someone, I'm assuming more of an expert than I am. My mind races with possibilities of what could have happened. Honestly, when I accepted the job, I thought it would be an adventure, but not actually dangerous. Maybe that was naive, or maybe we weren't in any real danger. It doesn't feel that way and when Simone returns to the truck, I lose it a little.

"Shel, are you okay?" she asks as my entire body begins to shake and my breaths are short. "Whoa there, big guy, give me your hands."

She grabs my hands and places my palms together,

rubbing calmly on the outside of them. My heart is racing and I think I'm sweating even more than I was before, which seems impossible.

"Look at me, Dr. Mini-perv." I do look at her and the panic recedes a bit, but I'm still in a full body shake. "Oh, fuck it," she says and then she's in my lap, straddling my trembling body.

Her hands grip the sides of my head and she puts her lips to mine. The pressure is insistent and her hands are firm on my jaw. Neither of us smell good, but it doesn't matter. I give in to her, to the sensation of the kiss. Her tongue breaches my lips as she ups the pressure and I let her in.

Eventually, I'm a full participant, my hands now in her hair, pulling her closer, not close enough. My heart is still pounding but now it's a steadier, headier pace. If I'm still shaking, it's because of her and how good she feels here, in my lap. We are completely wrapped around each other and I'm aware that we are in lotus, which is a good position for tantric sex. Let's just say my mind has been decidedly distracted.

Simone pulls back from the kiss and smiles at me. "Now, now," she scolds. "I didn't mean to do *that*." She points to my lap where I am most obviously aroused.

I give her a sheepish smile back and lean in to kiss her nose. "Thank you."

She unfolds herself from my lap and shoves me to the passenger side, taking over in front of the wheel.

"You're welcome. You have about 45 minutes to pull yourself together."

I lean my head back on the seat and close my eyes. "This has been an unusual day."

Her laugh is loud and unexpected. I raise my head and look at her. Her hair is askew and her shirt is covered in monkey hair, plastered to her with sweat. I've never seen a more beautiful woman in my life. She restarts the truck and carefully drives us back to the main road.

I must have fallen asleep after my adrenaline crash because I wake when the truck goes silent, with a bit of drool on my chin. Simone is still in the driver's seat looking at me warily.

"Are we okay, Doctor?"

I nod as I wipe my hand over my sweat and drool covered face.

"Here's what needs to happen, we are going to help unload Lala and her cub, make sure she and the cub don't have any pressing health needs, eat, shower, and then bed."

"I think I can manage those things," I say quietly.

Turns out I *can* manage those things. Before Lala and her cub can be released into a larger holding cage, I am able to do a basic health check and find them both to be in good shape, if not a little underfed. Once they are loaded into their temporary home, Simone and I head to the cantina for some food, rice and beans with some grilled eggplant. The food is surprisingly good and even though I'm not vegan I've been enjoying it.

"Does Beto do all the cooking?" I ask Simone who is chugging down a beer after cleaning her plate.

"Nigel also does some when Beto can't make it. You can always tell when Nigel makes something because it has curry in it and most likely raisins." She makes a face like raisins are the devil and then takes my empty plate to a bucket for cleaning.

"I'm headed to the shower and then I'm going to sleep like the dead, you joining me?" she asks and I blush.

"Um, sure," I say hesitating.

"Oh my lord, I'm not asking you to join me in the shower, Dr. Mini-perv, I am way too tired to deal with our lap shenanigans earlier." She pats my shoulder. "Come on, you look like you're barely keeping your eyes open."

She's right, I'm more tired than I've ever been in my life. I follow her back to our tent, we get our things, and head to the shower area

"So, tell me about Lala," I say as we step into separate stalls. The shower area is a series of stalls covered by a canvas roof, but open on all sides. Each shower has about a four-foot wall around it, If you want to see someone naked in the shower, you'd only need to step about a foot from their stall. There seems to be an honor system—when you enter the shower area, you take the furthest available so privacy remains. Simone takes the end shower stall and so I take the opposite end though we are still close enough for conversation.

Her face lights up and my heart drops to my stomach. "Oh, I'm so happy she's here. About six months ago, we rescued a lion and two of his male cubs. We knew the circus had female lions they were hiding from us, and that one was the lion's mate. His name is Felix and Lala is that mate."

"You've been searching for her, then?"

"Yes," she says as she rinses shampoo from her hair. I can just see the tops of her freckle dusted shoulders. "She must have been pregnant and that's why they hid her from us, her cub would be worth selling. I guess we ended up being the buyers. They made more than they would have, but lost a lion who sold tickets."

"They lost a baby monkey, too," I add.

"That they did." She leans back and my eyes lock on her delicate collarbone. Good thing I'm in this lukewarm shower with my raging hard-on. "I'll never get over people's need to own wild animals, not to mention their need for making them perform."

"From what I've read and from my talks with Nigel, it's certainly a complex issue here. Hopefully, the laws will remain and minds will change. It may take a while, but the world is changing."

"Yes, slower than I'd like but things are moving in the right direction." Her smile is more of a smirk but it's still beautiful. "We lucked out that the circus landed in Eric's town. It's going to change her life, and Felix is going to be happy again. He's at one of our facilities in Colorado so she'll head there in a few days. Nancy is already working on the logistics. I wish I could be there for their reunion."

"Ms. Lyon, are you a romantic?"

She laughs. "Of course I am, I rescue animals and deliver them to freedom. I'm nothing but romantic." She shuts the water off and grabs her towel from a hook in the corner of the stall.

I lose sight of her as she bends to dry off. I take the opportunity to finish washing myself and then turn the water off in my own stall.

"You say that like it's a character flaw. I find being a romantic akin to a love of life, its beauty and flaws."

"Oh brother, you are too much, Dr. DNA."

"I don't know what you mean by that," I respond because I don't. I have no idea at all what she thinks of me.

"I mean, it's hard to believe you are for real sometimes." She bends down wrapping the towel around her head. I watch, mesmerized as she takes a piece of clothing and then it disappears behind the shower stall. None of this makes my dick less hard.

Once I have my shorts on, I sling my towel over my shoulder and exit the stall. "I'm still at a loss, I *am* a real person."

She tilts her head at me, steps out of the stall, then takes a long perusal of my bare torso. Her finger drifts up and down, pointing at me.

"This is what I'm talking about. Your body is insane, and then you say things like romance is akin to a love of life." Her hands are on her hips now. "Men like you don't exist in real life. Ask pretty much any woman."

At this moment, Nancy walks in dressed in a silk robe, shower cap on her head. She looks at both of us and smiles a wide smile. "Look at you two, bunkmates, lion rescuers, and shower buddies. I knew I was right about you," she says pointing at me.

"Nancy, do men like me exist in real life?" I ask.

She puts her hands to her chest and gasps. "Dr. Locke, you stand before me, with this physique, this face, and the tender way you treat an animal and I dare say, no. Men like you certainly do not exist in real life. I barely believe my Nigel exists, but he does. Sadly, the two of you are not the norm, I wish I could say otherwise."

Simone nods, makes a 'see' face at me, and exits the shower area.

"I still don't know what that means," I say squinting against the setting sun as I watch her walk away.

Nancy pats my shoulder. "I believe they call you a unicorn. A kind, hot man with a job is rare, but one who is sensitive, loves animals, looks like an Adonis, and has proper equipment," she says with a wink, "is a unicorn."

"Thank you," I say. "I like to think I strive to be kind and am always improving. I'm just myself."

She sighs and turns on the water. "Keep being yourself, Dr. Locke, it's a pleasure to be witness to it."

When I get back to the tent, I text Suzy.

Me: *Do men like me exist in real life?*
Suzy: *Oh boy, are we fishing for compliments today, Shelbell?*
Me: *Not really, but I've had two women tell me today that I'm not real.*
Suzy: *You are definitely not like most men I know, but that's what makes you, you and them, them. It's not right or wrong either way.*
Me: *So I am abnormal?*
Suzy: *No, you are better than normal. You are smart, hot, and you care about people.*
Me: *Caring about people seems normal.*
Suzy: *You'd think. Just keep being you, Shel, you are one of the best people I know and you certainly do exist. You aren't perfect, but you are pretty amazing.*

Me: *Thanks, Suze, I really wasn't fishing but I needed to hear that from someone who has seen me make a mistake or two.*

Suzy: *Anytime, King Kong D!!*

Me: *You had to throw that in?*

Suzy: *May as well remind you of one of your best features!*

Me: *You do know how to boost my ego.*

Suzy: *It is quite impressive when it's boosted!*

Me: *On that note…talk soon!*

Suzy: *Yes! I love seeing all the pictures and adventure stories with those kitties! Keep sending emails.*

CHAPTER 7

MAN VS. BEAST

MY DAYS ARE PRETTY MUCH the same for about a week. Get up, eat breakfast, visit all of the cats, then go through the list of tasks by priority. The tigers with diarrhea have been a priority most days, as well as those with seizures. I spend the morning with Emilio and Gloria, observing how he functions with his injured lip.

"You should see the other guy," Simone says and startles me as I sit by the cage. "Oops, I did not mean to scare you, Dr. Mini-perv." This nickname has made a reappearance after she found me sculpting a series of figures performing oral sex yesterday in preparation for Emilio's surgery.

For most of the week, Simone and I have had little interaction. I've been busy preparing the cats for travel, and she has been supervising the arrival of the crates that will house each cat when we are flying to South

Africa. The crates are handmade in Guatemala by local tradesmen using specs patented by Freedom Roar. Nigel told me about how they were literally picking scrap metal from junkyards during their first rescue in Peru.

Maybe she's avoiding me, or maybe it's me avoiding her, or a little of both. I've also steered clear of Quique other than helping with feeding. He's the most formidable of the cats and I haven't decided how I want to approach him yet to see if we can be friends.

"It's okay," I assure her. "I'm procrastinating about my meeting with Quique, I have plenty of data about poor Emilio here."

She slaps me gently on the shoulder. "Okay, then, let's get you and the big guy together."

I sigh out a big breath and stand, stretching my arms over my head, swaying from side to side. As I lower my arms, I catch Simone looking low, where my shirt has ridden up. Her cheeks go red and I smile to myself. I've kept my distance because I don't want her to feel uncomfortable, but it's nice to know I affect her a little. I return the favor, staring at her ass encased lovingly in a pair of high waisted shorts.

Quique is lounging at the back of his enclosure, tail flipping back and forth. I examined his two male cubs yesterday and although they have a stiff-legged gait that are telltale signs of excess in-breeding, they are other-wise healthy and playful. I'm scheduled to look over his female family members later today with a local veterinarian who has been a huge help as he filled in before I arrived. Unfortunately, all of the females suffer from seizures.

"Hola, Quique…Quique, grande! Magnifico!" I call to him. "Bueno, Qui, bueno." I try to keep my voice soft and respectful. Sinking to my knees, I also bow my head slightly staring directly at him. He stares back and doesn't even blink, waiting for my next move.

I raise my head a little higher and then prop one knee in front of me. His head lifts a little higher, ears twitch. We continue to move one after the other, I put my hand on my hip, he stretches his haunches. I shift to a low crouch and he sits, looking like royalty. Eventually, both of us are standing and he steps a little closer to me. We stare at each other, him sizing me up, and me trying not to flinch whenever he moves.

This beautiful creature has faced many beatings in his life and has good reason to hate humans, men especially. Not only was he abused, but he watched other animals in his family face brutal beatings as well. No one can blame him for being wary of me. Staring into his eyes, I get a soul deep feeling for this animal and want to connect with him.

Slowly, I offer him the back of my hand at the edge of the bars of the cage. Quique gives it a good look, leans in for a sniff, and to my amazement chuffs and gently bumps my hand with his head.

"Bueno, Quique, magnifico," I repeat overwhelmed by the offering of friendship.

I turn and Simone is staring at me like I did something extraordinary. Smiling back, I let out a nervous laugh. At that, Quique suddenly rises up on his hind legs to his full height—much taller than my 6 feet—and lets out a half growl, half roar.

"Si, si, you are the boss," Simone calls to him and I swear he nods as he comes back down on all fours. "Well, that was impressive, Dr. Locke. You met the beast and even though he definitely won, you earned a few points."

I'm speechless and trying not to wet my pants as we walk away from his cage. Quique has taken me down a few pegs and I'm reminded how much power these animals have, despite their appearance of being tame.

"We are starting to get our shopping lists ready and you and I will be the ones to go to town for some supplies. Are you free now or did you have more prep for tomorrow's procedure?" Simone asks as my heartbeat returns to a normal pace as we make our way to the cantina.

"I am meeting with Dr. Reyes in a bit but then I have no other plans today. I'd love to go to the city, I have only driven through on my way here from the airport and I was mostly gripping on to the seat for dear life."

We walk into the cantina and she and I make salads from the table full of fresh ingredients. The food has been delicious, despite everything being vegan. Nancy told me that they had been vegan for years, because how can you run an organization that is all about saving animals while continuing to eat them. I see her point and as a kid, I was vegetarian with my parents. When I got to college and had access to everything, I went omnivore and never went back.

Simone smiles and gestures to my bowl. "After our errands, we can go to a restaurant," she says looking around, then leaning in to whisper, "and eat whatever we want."

My eyes widen and I smile back at her. I know she means we can eat meat and dairy products but my dirty mind goes directly to taking a bite out of her. This week every time I've come to our shared tent, she's been asleep, making her sweet Simone sleeping sounds. Needless to say, I've taken several quick cold showers and have had difficulty falling asleep. I'm not usually this much of a creep and have plenty of self-control. There's just something about her that throws me back to being a hormonal teen, everything about her fascinates me and turns me on.

"Hello?" she says waving her hand in front of me. "Usually the meat coma comes after you eat it."

I choke on a chickpea and laugh. "I'm looking forward to it. Even though the food here is amazing, the thought of something other than beans, rice, and veggies sent me into a trance."

"Good, finish up your lunch and I'll meet you in front in 20 minutes." She takes her salad and heads to the main tent, leaving me to eat alone and daydream of grilled meats.

We spend most of the afternoon scouring Guatemala City for every sprig of lavender or bottle of lavender oil in order to keep the tigers calm on our long flights. The other main items on our list are tongs and wheel-able coolers. The city is huge and split up into zones. Simone and I stay in zone one which is the main downtown area. Much of the area is paved in marble and is dotted with fancy hotels and restaurants. After hours of walking and haggling, we pack our items in our van and head back out to find food.

Simone leads me to a small hole in the wall place that she had been to on a previous trip. The menu was modern Mayan which was exactly the experience I was looking for. We ordered four different dishes, steak, shrimp, chicken, and pigeon—when in Guatemala! It was all served with unique sauces, fries, warm flatbread, avocados, yucca, and other grilled vegetables. I definitely ate too much and the four empty Gallo bottles mean I also drank too much beer.

I don't regret a minute.

"Is it possible to die from overeating?" Simone asks arching back in her chair, hand to her stomach.

"That's surely possible, have you not seen *Monty Python's The Meaning of Life*?" I answer, patting my stomach in solidarity.

"It's only a wafer-thin mint," she says in a high-pitched British accent.

I laugh. "That's a yes, then."

She nods. "When your father is a Brit and thinks he's a comedian, then yes, you've watched everything that Monty Python has released, ever. Nigel is a huge fan as well, fair warning to not get him started or you'll be drowning in *Life of Brian* quotes for days."

"Noted. I guess I shouldn't tell you that I have a series of miniatures of characters from *The Holy Grail*?"

"Oh, good googly moogly, I'm surrounded." She is teasing me but her smile is warm, the flutter in my heart makes me warm too.

"Did you say googly moogly?" I lean in, my tone serious.

"I did, you ridiculous nincompoop."

We stay silent for a beat and then burst into laughter. What she said was not particularly funny but sometimes you just have to be there and then crack up because why keep it in?

"Thanks for bringing me here, I needed a little normal day out and some animal protein." I reach for her hand and she lets me hold it and give it a squeeze.

"You're welcome," she says squeezing my hand back then releasing it. "Now, let's get some ice cream." She stands and throws a pile of quetzals on the table.

I follow her out and we walk a few blocks to a place that has ice cream rolls—I know it's confusing but the ice cream is served rolled up, not in scoops. I order chocolate and Simone gets pistachio and it's some of the best ice cream I've had.

"This is weird but really good," I say.

"That is exactly what I think of you," she jokes. "You are weird but also a really good dude."

I scrape the bottom of my nearly empty cup, not sure how to proceed with this line of conversation. We've had a great day, chatting about the logistics of our future trip and the health of the cats and then dinner. Dinner was more personal, I found out a bit more about her, and told her a few vet stories. Since then, there's been a flirty undercurrent and maybe it's just my tipsy brain, but I think Simone likes me and I say that out loud.

"You like me."

"What's not to like? You are smart, funny, built like Thor, and you care about animals. If I was a relationship girl, I'd put a ring on it ASAP."

"You're not a relationship girl?" I ask, ignoring all the nice stuff she said, tossing my empty cup in the trash.

"Ugh, no, and there are too many reasons to why that is. I won't bore you."

"But, you still like me." I poke her shoulder.

"You are too much, I do like you but don't get your hopes up about any more lap shenanigans with me. That was a one-time thing in order to calm your ass down."

I step in closer to her, crowding her against the other wall of the ice cream shop. "I haven't been calm around you since that day in the truck. Whatever you thought you were doing had the opposite effect. I can't stop thinking about you on my lap and how to get you back there." She sighs and leans into my chest for a second before pushing her hand on my chest. I immediately back off.

"I'm sorry, was that too much?" I ask. Maybe I read her signals wrong and am coming on too strong?

She shakes her head. "No, I'm the one who should be sorry. I've been all over the place since we've met. I thought for sure you'd invite me to your room that night but you didn't. In retrospect, I'm happy you didn't because it would have been awkward, but I still feel a little rejection sting from it."

"If I didn't need to get up at 4 am to catch my flight I would have asked you. No rejection at all—just me being nervous about the job—what I feel now is regret, because even though it would have been awkward, I'd still have the memory of you wrapped around me."

She covers her face with her hands. "Great googly moogly," she mumbles and I draw her into a hug and she nestles into my chest.

CHAPTER 8

MISSION IMPOSSIBLE 2

TWO DAYS after our trip to the city I am hit with a double whammy.

I wake up early this fine Sunday morning and decide to spend it with my favorite tigers, Tasha and Kamal. I've been able to give them some medication for their bowel issue and have put some fiber into their diet. My hope is they will be able to have a solid poop before we put them on an airplane.

"Hola, muchacho y muchacha. Tasha, bonita." I call them gently and they wander over to the front of their enclosure to sniff me and then they both chuff at me. Tasha lets me scratch and pet her head and ears and is the sweetest girl. I'm so engrossed in giving her scratches that I don't notice what Kamal is doing.

When tigers are ready to go to the bathroom, they do a little dance and start backing up their haunches. This has been a telltale sign when dealing with Kamal and Tasha and their explosive expressions since I've arrived and I know to get clear of the splash zone. My only excuse is that I was feeling a real connection with Tasha and it was a nice moment. Then it wasn't.

My first clue should have been Tasha jumping back from the bars. It all happened so fast though. I was petting her, she was gone and when I turned my head —blammo!

Tigers have diarrhea just like everyone else. It's watery, horrid smelling, and projects out of his anus like a powerful stream of urine. When I say horrid smelling, it's like rotting meat on top of a pile of sewage, topped with some regurgitated bad fish—and that's when you are cleaning it off the ground with a whole lot of sawdust and a rake. When it lands mere inches from your face, more specifically on your torso, it's a whole new level.

There's tiger shit dripping down my body as I quickly get out of range and take my shirt, pants and shoes off. I throw the clothes away and put my boots to the side to see if they can be salvaged. When Simone finds me five minutes later, I'm only in my soon to be trash boxer briefs heading to the showers.

"Oh shit!" she exclaims when she sees me.

"Yep," I say because what else is there to say really? I duck into the shower area and into the first stall I see, turning the water on as hot as I can stand it. Once I'm fully under, I drop my underwear and kick it as far away as I can.

Belatedly, I realize I have nothing. No soap, shampoo, towel or clothes. I'm still just rinsing literal shit off my body when I hear Simone clear her throat. When I turn, she is handing me my shower bag, clean clothes and a towel.

"Thanks, I wasn't thinking ahead after being brutally assaulted by a tiger's asshole. My only thought was to get it off immediately." I wash my hands thoroughly with the soap before washing the rest of me.

Simone laughs. "I'm sorry, I'm really trying to hold it in but it's so hard." She then bends at the waist, continuing to belly laugh at my fecal misfortune.

"Oh dios mio," I hear and turn to see Rico, Nancy and Nigel coming to stand with Simone. Nancy has the good manners to cover her face as she laughs at me, but Nigel and Rico are slapping their knees and holding each other up.

"Oh, a regular chuckle fest, eh?" I say, trying to see the humor in it, but I'm pretty sure I got some tiger shit in my mouth. My. Mouth. "Won't be so funny after I use all the hot water for today."

"Dude, you deserve every last drop," Simone says and they all continue to laugh.

"Maybe once I have all the liquid shit washed off my body and out of my mouth, I'll see the humor." I gag a little and grab my toothpaste, squeezing out a line on my finger and jamming it in my mouth.

The crowd has grown by the time I finish scrubbing every last corner of my body like I was washing off toxic waste. Now in addition to Nigel, Nancy, Rico, and Simone, there are Beto, Sal, two volunteers that came to help feed the tigers today and Dr. Reyes the local vet.

"Where is Diego? Seems like the only one missing out on my shame," I say, now toweling myself off.

"Ayy, did I miss the caca?" Diego says as he walks up next to Simone, who is still in semi-hysterics.

"The caca is still out there near Kamal's cage if you are interested," I say helpfully.

Nigel tuts and everyone calms down a little. "Now, let's all get our shit together, and meet in the cantina in 15, I have an announcement. I know you all must be pooped from waking up so early, but I think a little bit of the brown can help that."

They all try to keep from laughing but when I step out and try to pass them, they all start up again, patting me on the back.

"Yeah, yeah, what a bunch of comedians." I get past them and finally make it to my tent. I find a pair of tennis shoes I brought along and throw them on with some socks. Simone brought me cargo pants and a t-shirt and I add a zip up hoodie because I feel like I want to be as covered as possible.

When I arrive at the cantina, I get a round of

applause and some wolf whistles, then it dies down as we sit and eat oatmeal and drink the "brown" coffee Nigel was alluding to.

He stands and taps his spoon on his mug. "I have an announcement."

"Yes, we know dear, you told us that," Nancy interrupts and I'm happy to have someone else be made fun of for five seconds.

He gives her a smile and then looks at me. "Oh yes, whilst we all watched Dr. Locke wash the stench from his body."

I roll my eyes and secretly like the attention.

"As I was saying, we have another mission!" he exclaims, clapping his hands together.

My heart drops through my stomach as he explains in detail the three lion cubs we will be rescuing from a circus three hours away.

On the list of other things I don't want to do again, throwing up out of a truck window with the woman I like sitting next to me is high up there. Yet here I am, on another rescue mission because I can't say no. It's bad enough she saw me drenched in tiger shit just hours ago, now she has to witness the second showing of my lunch.

We are about an hour into our three-hour trek and the motion sickness pills I took are finally kicking in. Thank goodness because there wasn't much left to lose.

I swish my mouth with some warm water and then spit it out the window, in one of my most unattractive moves. Before the trip, I had some forethought and packed a Gatorade and some gum. Small sips of the drink and a cool breeze filtering through the window bring some relief and I feel about 50% myself.

"How can we get three new cubs ready for transport in three days?" I ask since our big trip is looming and there's a ton to do for the cats we already have under our care.

Simone gives me a look. "Wellll, I was on my way to tell you when the whole poop incident took precedence over everything." She and I laugh a little. Yes, I can laugh a little about it now that I can't still taste it in my mouth. My stomach rolls at the thought and maybe I can't think about it just yet. "Our permits fell through to land in the US so we are postponing so we can reroute."

"Postponing for how long?" I ask, knowing we are on a time crunch with the government.

"Just another ten days. It cuts it close to the deadline but we will make it work, we always do." Her hands are tight on the steering wheel as she looks intently forward.

"It must be nerve-wracking though when so much is on the line."

"You'll see how it's all worth it when we get to South Africa," she says turning to me with a smile. "You should take a little nap before we get there, since you'd already had a harrowing day."

I nod, lean my head against my rolled up hoodie, and pass out.

When I wake, the truck is stopped and I'm alone. Quickly I look out the window and see Simone, Nigel, Nancy, and Rico all in a huddle. The landscape is green and I can see a mountain in the distance. We are headed to a town called Gualán where the circus has apparently been for a few weeks.

Dragging myself out of the truck is a good thing to do because I've been in there for a few hours. I regret doing it too quickly because I get lightheaded and nearly fall over.

"Whoa there, mate," I hear Nigel say and feel his arm around my torso to keep me upright. My vision is fuzzy and my ears are ringing but it doesn't last more than a couple of seconds and then I'm okay. "Here," he says handing me a bottle of cold water, "drink this and we'll get you something to eat."

The cool water feels like heaven on my dry and irritated throat. The mention of food reminds me how empty my stomach is from all the coming so I look forward to anything he offers.

My food options are a vegan protein bar or a bag of plain unsalted popcorn. I take both although neither sounds appetizing. At least the bar has sunflower seed in it to add some flavor so I eat it in two bites. I'm grazing on the popcorn when I finally am able to focus on what they're discussing. This rescue is different because we are preparing for three lions instead of one and we've brought our own cages this time since they've dealt with the owner before and he refuses to relinquish any more property than his cats.

"He must have hidden the cubs from us," I hear Nancy say. "When we got Kamal and Tasha there was no sign of them."

"They were probably small enough to be kept in one of the residential trailers. Let's not have a go at ourselves for things we can't change. We know about them now and we will get them." Nigel reassures Nancy.

"The local police and town officials are meeting us there so we will hopefully have more cooperation this time." Rico doesn't sound convinced as he makes this statement, but at least it won't be a grandma with a gun scenario.

Simone looks at me. "Sheldon, we will mostly need your help moving crates this time so you won't have to be involved with any negotiation. Hopefully, there won't be any pressing vet needs but if there is, you're on." She turns to Rico. "We will let you speak for the most part unless you give us a signal otherwise. Our limit for the three is 15 but I'd like to keep it to 10 if we can. Unfortunately, this guy knows us and that we will pay to get the animals, so we are expecting push back until an offer is made."

Simone told me the first time that the circus owners

are supposed to be reimbursed by the government for surrendering their animals but it's not very much and there's a lot of red tape to go through for them to receive the funds. Freedom Roar made the decision to offer them cash to expedite the process and because even though many of the circuses are horribly cruel to their animals, they depend on the income and it can be a hardship for their family and employees. It's a complicated world we live in and my hope is that these people will be able to find another way to make money without harming animals.

The discussion goes on another few minutes and I learn we are about 30 minutes from our destination. We stopped so everyone could chat at once, use the "restroom" and stretch their legs.

"Why don't you drive?" Simone asks.

"Thank you," I say because she knows I tend to have less motion sickness when I drive and it will distract me from being nervous.

We pull behind Rico in the smaller truck to follow and the road is pretty empty which makes me feel more comfortable driving the big flatbed.

"What is your practice like at home?" Simone asks.

"I split a clinic with two other vets in the Sunset district of San Francisco. It's a very busy place and I'm one of two exotics vets but I'd say my days are full of neutering cats and dogs normally. I get the occasional sick turtle, snake, or hedgehog, but for the most part, it's dog and cat checkups with some rabbits, guinea pigs, and hamsters thrown in a few times a week."

"What animal do you like the most?"

"Dogs."

"I mean, I would have lied and said cats since you're helping the big ones, but go with dogs, my friend."

"I like cats too but dogs are my favorite."

"Why?"

"They are loyal, eager to please, and are true companions. Cats are great they just are more aloof and have sharper claws and teeth."

"Fair enough, what's your least favorite?"

"Birds."

"No elaboration?"

"Birds are extraordinary and I do appreciate them in the wild. They are depressing as pets though."

"Favorite food?"

"Tacos."

"Same here. Favorite dessert?"

"Ice cream."

"I'm a cake girl but I do appreciate a good ice cream roll." She winks at me and we both smile. "Favorite TV show?"

"*New Girl.*"

She laughs at my answer and I get it, it's not the typical dude show, but I love it.

"Seriously?"

"Yes, especially the first three seasons. The chemistry, little nuances, and one-liners that you almost don't hear kill me."

"I'm sure Zooey Deschanel isn't too hard to look at either."

"Got me there, but I'm more of a Cece fan."

She rolls her eyes. "The tall, voluptuous model is your fave? Shocker."

"Book?"

"*The Hobbit.*"

"Movie?"

"*Vertigo.*"

"Oh, good choice, I love that movie. Have you seen it at the Castro?" she asks.

I nod. "Yeah, I've been a few times. It's a long movie to watch on those seats, especially when you're as big as me."

"I saw *My Fair Lady* there and even though there was an intermission I still had numb ass for days."

"Do you live in the city?" I ask, realizing I never asked her where she lives.

"I have an apartment in Berkeley but I travel so much I live there maybe half the year. The Freedom Roar offices are in downtown Oakland but I do spend a good amount of time in San Francisco. What part of the city do you live in?"

"I live in the Inner Sunset by the park. It took me forever to find my place but I love it. It's a two bedroom on 4th and Hugo St. I'm close to the Haight, the park and I can ride my bike to work. Plus, I got it for a steal because it was a gut job. Fortunately, my friend, Joe renovates for a living and he gave me a good deal. I had fun helping too."

"Wow, owning a home in the city, you're even more of a unicorn than previously thought." She pinches my elbow lightly. "Okay, favorite guilty pleasure?"

"None, because I refuse to feel guilty about something I like," I say echoing my mother who, you remember, raised me with no shame. "My favorite pleasure is sex."

"I almost forgot, you are shame-proof."

I nod as I follow Rico through the streets of a small town to the outskirts where we pull into a small parking lot near an outdoor arena that probably seats about a thousand people. We sit in the truck, as Nigel told us not to get out until all was clear. Whatever that means.

"Pennywise, come in, Pennywise, Candyman here, over." The squawk of the walkie-talkie puts me on alert.

"Go for Pennywise, over," Simone responds.

"We are good to go for operation Hakuna Matata, over." Nigel is like a giant child and there's something about his joy for saving these animals that is contagious. Despite the ridiculous nicknames and mission names, he is very serious about his work.

"It's show time," Simone says before she hops out of the truck.

CHAPTER 9

THE LYON SLEEPS

SIMONE LYON SLEEPS like the dead—a noisy dead, but once she's asleep it's near impossible to wake her up. We are all exhausted after a long day of driving, negotiating with people and then lions in order to get them to move from one cage to another. Fortunately, we had plenty of food to lure them, but they must have just been fed because it took a lot of goading. The owner of the circus, on the other hand, was more agreeable. Nigel ended up paying him 12,000q for the cubs which seemed like a fair amount to me but what do I know.

It's well after midnight and I am bone tired but cannot fall asleep. Partly from left over adrenaline from the rescue, and partly because of the woman snoring as loud as a chainsaw not three feet from me.

Watching her navigate, not just today's events but crisis after crisis here at camp, whether it's volunteers not showing up or our flight needing to be rearranged through a new country, she barely breaks a sweat. Her confidence and ability to solve near impossible problems makes me want to grab her and do all sorts of dirty things. Sure, she's a beautiful woman aesthetically, but her dedication to these cats, and the people who are here helping, makes her glow from the inside.

I need to get out of this tent before I do something unwise like stare too long at her and have her wake up and catch me. My skin feels too tight and I am craving motion. I slide on some sweat pants and a hoodie, along with my now diarrhea free boots—thanks to Diego— and head out of the tent.

There are solar lights around the encampment pathways but I have my flashlight as well. I walk away from where the cats are because they are locked down with extra protection at night and I wouldn't want to disturb them anyway.

I walk past the cantina and the main tent to the paved area where all of the vehicles are. After the cubs were unloaded, I examined each one more thoroughly and found them to be pretty healthy, more so than any other cat already in residence. While I was doing this, Rico and Nigel washed the flatbed of lion urine, feces, and vomit. I know this because Nigel spoke about the glamour of saving the animals at dinner. The cubs, like me, were suffering from motion sickness and threw up several times.

Climbing onto the flat bed, I can see it's still damp so I climb up on top of the cab of the truck and sit with my legs dangling over the windshield. Leaning back, I stare at the starry sky on this clear and mild night. Stars are pretty visible since we are far enough from the city. When I was growing up on the farm, the star gazing was epic. We were out in the boonies and our farm was dark at night.

My dad and I used to sit on top of our tractor and look through a telescope to see all sorts of stars, planets and moons. If I wasn't so obsessed with animals, I probably would have become an astrophysicist. Science will always be my number one love. I make a promise to myself to call my parents tomorrow. They finally got a cell phone (just one to share), and being here makes me miss them. I lay all the way back, cradling my head just enjoying the view.

"Psst, Shel," someone whisper yells, and by someone, I mean Simone. I lean up on my elbow and give her a little wave. "What are you doing up there?"

"Looking at the sky," I whisper yell back. "Come on up."

She gracefully jumps up onto the bed and then takes my offered hand, swinging up to land next to me, hip to hip. When I lay back, she goes with me. I can smell her shampoo from showering before bed. It smells like french toast, maple vanilla maybe? Whatever it is, I like it.

With my hands behind my head, she has no choice but to rest on my arm and does so without hesitation. There's been a delicate tension between us these past few weeks but we enjoy each other's company. We are comfortable together, whether we are working, eating, or relaxing in our tent. The closeness I feel to her is real, and the physical closeness now is something I am enjoying.

"Some day, huh?" she says and I turn my head to see her wry smile.

"You could say that it's been one of the more eventful of my stay here."

"Hey, you started the day sprayed in shit, but ended with lion cub snuggles." Her hand lands on my abdomen and I stop breathing.

"Those snuggles were almost as good as the Simone snuggle I'm getting right now," I say and her hand slides across my body to settle on my side, her completely turned into me. I move my arm behind her head and pull her in closer.

"In theory, you shouldn't be good at it because you are so hard and muscle-y, but you are surprising me with your stellar ability to nestle me in and keep me comfy." She looks at me as I tilt my head to her. Her lips are close and tempting. "Do you want to kiss me, Shel?" she whispers.

"Yes, I really do want that," I say, brushing my lips over her cheek to plant a gentle kiss on her nose. "Do you want me to kiss you, Simone?"

"I think it would be an even better ending to this day than lion cub snuggles."

I laugh a little but stop when she leans up and places her lips on mine. This kiss is different from the others we've shared. The first was barely even worth noting except for our mouths touching. The second was soothing, primal, and necessary. This kiss is necessary in a different way. I need to kiss her because I've thought of little else, and because she asked. I'm aware that both of the other kisses were instigated by her, but I don't think there was anything behind her instigations other than impulse. This kiss is purposeful and different—or I'm just reading more into it like I always do.

I deepen the kiss, moving my hand to cup her face and turning to her. Her lips are soft and she tastes like toothpaste and delicious woman. Each woman has a distinct taste when you kiss her, despite anything she just ate or drank. It's like her essence, but really just saliva. Now I'm making it a little gross and technical, but it is chemistry in the end, isn't it?

Whatever magic is in Simone's mouth, is undeniable. I could spend hours kissing her and not get tired of it. She grips my shirt and throws her leg over mine, so I go deeper and thread my hand through her hair, pulling slightly. I swallow her gasps and moans, while trying to get her as close to me as possible.

When we break apart, she's a vision, swollen lips,

flushed freckles, and so much heat in her eyes. I nibble along her jaw and down to her neck. I pause where her shoulder and throat meet, inhaling her scent, moving my lips over her skin.

"Shel, wait," she says and I still my lips at her throat. I'm worried she is stopping me, but instead, she presses on my shoulder so I'm again on my back. She follows me, straddling my lap and laying across me, her hands draped past my shoulders. Leaning in she kisses me again as I slide my hands to her hips, gripping her there, pulling her closer.

My dick is rock solid and I'm not sure she notices until she rocks back a little. "Jesus," she says panting. "That ought to be illegal."

"It is in 13 states," I joke and she buries her face under my chin, giggling. My arms go around her and I sit up, keeping her in my lap, her legs on either side of my torso, mine dangling over the roof of the cab. "Can I keep kissing you? I thought you were adamant about the lap shenanigans yet here we are."

She nods her head and I lean down to kiss her chest. Her top is vee neck and I pull it down slightly kissing the tops of her breasts, then working my way back up to her luscious mouth. Pausing there, my eyes on hers, I pull back.

"What's wrong?" she asks.

"Nothing," I whisper, but I'm a liar. "You are so beautiful, and I can't for the life of me figure out how you think I'm remotely attractive after being shit on in the morning and then vomiting in the afternoon. It's a wonder I guess."

She laughs, throwing her head back. "It is a wonder. You've had a day, that's for sure, but it's all of that happening, and you still show up, no complaints, and do your job. You literally wash the shit off and keep going. Not to mention, those disgusting things get wiped away when my last visual is you cradling a lion cub shirtless. That type of thing goes a long way."

"I don't want to mess things up, and I am famous for doing that."

"How do you mess things up?" she asks, her hands at my nape, playing with my hair.

"Well, I think the biggest mistake I make is coming on too strong, and then having sex with a woman too soon."

"How soon is too soon?"

I cringe, knowing that this may turn her off. "My usual pattern, according to my friend, Frank, and myself when I have things in perspective, is I meet a woman, find her interesting, and then try to keep her by offering sex."

She tilts her head and narrows her eyes. "How often do they accept the offer?"

I sigh, leaning my forehead to hers.

"Can you give me a ballpark?" she asks, her voice still light.

I lean back and look her in the eyes. "More than I want to admit, and hopefully less than your worst-case scenario. My friend, Suzy, also my longest relationship at about a month, teases me because I always practice safe sex, just not safe heart. I go in with the best of intentions and it never works."

"So every date you go on, you end up sleeping with the person?"

"A date, or someone I meet at a party, or at a coffee shop, or a hotel bar," I say the last one so she knows my original intention. "I love women, and unfortunately, I fall in love with them quickly, or so I think. I try too hard, jump the gun, and end up alone."

"Wow, that's kind of sad, but you seem self-aware about it. Is it something you've been working on?"

"Yeah, there was someone recently that I thought was the one for me. We went on a few dates, and had sex each time. Maybe it's my free upbringing, but I don't have any hang-ups about sex. I don't devalue it, and when I am in it, I'm completely there, and I take it seriously." I lean back onto the truck roof and Simone rolls off of me but tucks herself back to my side. "She also was very sexual, but unfortunately, not just with me. I thought we were exclusive, I was wrong. She said it was just sex, but it wasn't for me, I cared about her, spent time with her, and was sincerely interested in her. It messed me up so I went to a therapist and she helped me think about my life objectively, and to explore my behaviors and why I do what I do."

"That's good, Shel, I hope you realize you can't take all the blame, right?"

"I guess not. The women I'm with always give consent so I know they want to have sex with me. My mistake is thinking they want me for more than my physical body."

"It's really their mistake, because although your body is spectacular, it's your dedication to animals, kindness, grit, and weirdness that make me want you."

"You want me?" I ask, there goes the keeping it cool.

She laughs and turns my head to look at her. "Yes, but now that I know your tendencies, I'm thinking you should wait."

"Fair enough, but make no mistake that I want you too. Whenever you're ready."

I feel the loss of her warmth as she sits up, swings her legs around and hops down to the truck bed. When I sit up and turn, she's climbing down from the bed to the ground and gives me a wave.

"Goodnight, Doctor." She gives me a salute and skips back towards the tents.

When I return to the tent later, she is blissfully snoring with a smile on her face.

CHAPTER 10

RULES ARE RULES

THE NEXT MORNING, I spend some time with the new cubs and then I sit in the office with my miniatures to keep my hands warmed up. Today is Emilio's surgery and I want to be at my best. Simone was out of the tent before I woke up and I haven't seen her all morning. Nancy told me she went with Nigel to the airport to deal with some permits. Our new flight date is a week from today and it's a mere two days before the regime change that makes our trip time sensitive.

"It's like you are making up these positions at this point. That's not real, no one bends that way," Simone sits across from me, pointing to the pair of lovers I'm currently working on.

"I assure you that the windmill is a legit Kama Sutra position," I answer her while concentrating fully on the two figures I am working on. The man is on top with his legs on either side of the woman's torso facing away from her, he enters her this way and slides back and forth. "It's difficult and the man needs to be decently endowed, but it's definitely real."

When I look up, Simone's face is flushed and she is giving me a knowing look. "Tried it have you? I feel like you are just bragging with these creations now. You could make anything but you choose these dirty little vignettes to torture me."

"The last thing I want is to torture you," I say, adding a vein to the man's erect penis. "Maybe you should be looking inward at your archaic views on sexuality." I'm teasing her and she's smart enough to not take the bait.

"Or maybe you should prepare yourself physically and mentally for all the ideas you've planted in my sex brain, while creating literal porn in front of me."

"Hmm, sex brain? Is that a real thing?"

"Sure, it's the best part of most brains." She picks up a pair in standing lotus, admiring my work. "Right now, I have food brain though so I'm headed to the cantina, want to join me?"

I nod. "Let me finish this and I'll meet you there, a salad sounds good before Emilio's surgery."

"You need sustenance for all the standing," she says looking closer at the pair in her hands. She whispers, "Unreal."

"Oh, Shel, you and your filthy miniature sex addicts.

I don't know whether to wash your mouth out with soap, or hug you." Nancy drifts in and sets herself on the desk next to mine.

"Maybe a spanking," Simone says and everything goes quiet.

"Uh," I stammer as Nancy bursts into laughter. Simone and I look at each other and follow Nancy's lead.

After we settle down, Simone says she'll meet me in the cantina and leaves the tent. I'm carefully placing my small works of art in their protective case while Nancy watches me with a raised eyebrow.

"I wanted to make sure I was prepared for Emilio," I say and she nods but the eyebrow remains.

"You're prepared, I'm sure. My worry is that you aren't prepared for that one," she says throwing a thumb in the direction of Simone.

"I hope you don't have to worry, but all the preparation in the world wouldn't prepare me for her."

"You know, we have rules about such folly but no one pays them any mind."

"Rules?" I ask a pit forming my stomach.

Nancy laughs. "Yes, the main rule is to treat her with respect and no breaking hearts."

"Ah, those sorts of rules. I will try my best to not mess it all up."

"I'm certainly looking forward to sitting back and

watching you two muddle through it." She puts her glasses on and turns to her paperwork. I'm dismissed.

The surgery with Emilio goes well and I'm satisfied that his quality of life will improve. With the injury to his mouth, he was having a hard time eating and drinking, affecting his weight and energy. He is still sedated and we're giving him some IV nutrients while we can. Unfortunately for Emilio, he will be on soft foods for a few days and will probably hate it.

After the surgery, I head to my tent to lie down for a bit. The hyper focus and physical stamina takes a toll and I need a cat nap (pun intended).

Simone is lounging in her cot reading when I enter, her eyes flick to me and then back to her book.

"How's my big guy?" she asks.

"I'm feeling great, thanks, a little tired, but otherwise I'm aces." She shakes her head at me and my lame joke as I lay myself down. "I'm shocked you didn't ask about Emilio, who is doing just fine. You should show more dedication to the animals," I tease, barely getting the last part out before she tackles me on my cot, holding my arms over my head, trying to tickle me. Sadly for her, I am not ticklish so her attack is futile.

"Ack!" she screeches, as I turn the tables and release my hands so I can dig my fingers into her sides.

"I wonder if this is against the rules?" I ask gripping her waist, stilling the wiggles. Her hands filter through my hair as she gives me a questioning look.

"Do you have rules, Shel?"

"Nah, and that's what gets me into trouble most of the time. I'm talking about the camp rules."

She smiles and shakes her head. "Did Nancy tell you about our no fraternization policy?"

I sit up, taking her with me, her poised for lap shenanigans. "She didn't and insinuated that there was no such policy."

"Don't look so worried, Doctor, after all, I'm the one who writes policy for the organization. Do you really think I'd go against a rule I wrote myself? Trust me, you aren't that irresistible." She pinches my cheek and I dig into her side again, causing her to giggle.

"You seem like the rebellious type, and there hasn't been that much resistance, to be honest." I lean in and kiss the side of her delectable mouth.

I don't have a lot of preference when it comes to women, I don't have a type, per se, but if I was pressed, I'd describe someone like Simone. She's a natural beauty and not very fussy. Not that our current living situation lends to fussiness, but she doesn't strike me as the type to worry over her looks overmuch. Her fiery hair is thick and although is in a ponytail for the majority of the day, because we are roommates, I get to see it released in all its glory. She takes meticulous care of her skin, but I imagine that's because she needs to protect her pale complexion from the sun. I catch her applying sunscreen constantly, and if I'm lucky I catch her lotioning up at bedtime. She's quite low maintenance and her natural beauty continues to throw me for a loop.

"How could I resist you, charming Dr. DNA?" She pokes my chest with her finger. "You have these puppy dog soulful eyes, this ridiculous lazy smile," she says pressing her lips to mine, "this body that keeps me up at night, and finally this." She presses her hands over where my heart lies in my chest. "You are a good man, despite your 'ho-ish ways."

The look in my eyes must convey what I want because she leans into me and puts her mouth to mine. Her sweet tongue breaches my lips and we drink at each other, kissing with a passion that seems different from the other times.

"Ding ding ding," I hear someone call from outside of our tent. "Kids, it's time for dinner," Nigel says in his deep booming voice. "We are having jackfruit tacos so get a move on."

Simone rolls her eyes. "We'll be there in a minute, Nige."

"Are jackfruit tacos something to get excited about?" I ask as she disengages from my cot and mosquito net.

"Most certainly not," she says, "tacos are meant to

be filled with carne asada or carnitas. These are a substitute and that's all the comment I can make about it."

"You seem upset," I say smiling. "Come with me to the city tomorrow morning, and we can get real tacos for lunch."

"Listen, Shel, I already said I'd sleep with you eventually, no need to make it more difficult to wait."

"Is that a yes?" I ask, putting on my hoodie.

"Yes, let's go eat completely unsatisfying vegan tacos tonight and dream of the meaty tacos of tomorrow. At least there will be avocados." She smacks my ass and leaves the tent.

The city is bursting in the morning, a much different experience than being here in the afternoon and early evening. Simone and I hit up Mercado Central, an underground market, looking for more lavender. I don't mean a secret market, no, this one is literally under the ground and kind of like an open-air market but without the air.

There are rows of stalls overflowing with items, everything from fruit and vegetables, to pork rinds the size of your head, to colorful candles and bags. We fill two bags with lavender and my backpack with avocados. Those are for the people, not the cats. Simone buys me a hat and I find the perfect gift for her as well.

"Is this what I think it is?" she asks, her eyes wide, mouth open in shock.

"If you're thinking it's a miniature knight that looks exactly like a knight who says 'Ni,' then you are correct." I found a stall with a corner full of miniatures of animals, boats, and strangely, knights with black armor like in the *Holy Grail*.

"This is my most cherished item from now until eternity," she shouts.

"Seems like an overreaction but I'll take it." I grab her hand and we wind our way out of the market back out to the street. We walk for a few blocks and stop in front of a white building with a mural of two colorful masked wrestlers competing for a delicious taco while a Day of the Dead skeleton watches.

"This is the perfect taco spot, when I was here a few months ago it was only Nancy and me and she loves shrimp but won't eat it around Nigel, so she brought me here." The sign says Mr. Taco and is colorful and when we step inside it smells divine.

Simone orders for both of us since her Spanish is better, and then we take our drinks and sit in the back area outside. The music is classic rock which I find jarring but comforting at the same time. We stow our shopping bags under the table and I relax in my chair.

"I forget how exhausting just walking around shopping in a city can be. This whole trip is the most tired I've been in my life but in a good way. I feel like at the end of each day I've done something important."

"You don't feel that way sometimes in your clinic?"

I shrug. "Sure, it's just different, spaying some hipster's French bulldog doesn't feel the same as preparing beleaguered lions and tigers to live out their days in peace after years of mistreatment." I sip my soda and Simone laughs.

"It's fulfilling work, for sure. Sometimes it feels like a slog but when we do the freedom days, releasing the cats into their forever homes of tall grasses and endless space to stretch out, there's no feeling like it." I look at Simone closely and the expression of caring and joy on her face shines through.

"Tell me more about you," I say because she's such a good listener, I feel like I'm prattling on all the time.

"You know the basics, I'm an East Bay girl, went to the East coast for college, and came right back since I'm definitely a California girl. Started working for Nigel and Nancy right out of college and am generally too busy for friends or relationships. My best friend is my college roommate, Valerie and she lives in New York. I see her every Thanksgiving and 4th of July—two holidays my dad refuses to celebrate."

"I like your dad, he sounds delightful."

"He's the opposite, a complete grumpier as Nigel would say, bloody tosser, that one."

We laugh as our tacos arrive and all becomes silent

as we inhale the world's most perfect food. My phone beeps interrupting the silence and I stare at the message for a long time trying to figure out if it's real.

Nigel: *Mayday, Krueger, you are needed at the Autosafari Chapin to assist in a hippo birth.*

Simone slows her chewing and tilts her head.

"This is by far the strangest text I've received," I say and hand her my phone.

She gasps and starts jumping in her seat. "I know where this is, and holy shit I'm gonna get to see a newborn hippo!" She squeals, jams the remaining taco in her mouth, followed by a generous gulp of iced tea, throws some quetzals on the table, and drags me out of the restaurant.

CHAPTER 11

HUNGRY HIPPO

HIPPOS ARE NOT to be trifled with on a normal day. Approaching one in labor is near suicidal. When Simone and I arrive at the large zoo-like place right outside of the city, I can hear the hippo mother's bellowing from the parking lot. My time working at a zoo included two hippos and they terrified me.

"Did you know that hippos are the second most deadly animals in Africa after the mosquito and tsetse fly?" I ask Simone. She looks more worried than I feel.

"Are you serious?"

"Yes, they are extremely territorial and can charge and crush humans easily. They can also drown you by knocking your boat over."

"They must be a delight while giving birth." I laugh, because there's little that's delightful about hippos. Sure, they have that so ugly they're cute thing going on, but they are brutal.

"Normally, they give birth in water, not sure what the setup is here," I say as we check in with a ticket taker and they call someone to let them know we are here. "The baby is born then swims to the surface for air. I've only seen a video of a hippo birth, never been there for the real thing. I'd be more excited if I wasn't so scared."

Simone laughs. "I'll make sure to take a lot of video then," she says. "For scientific purposes of course, not for your potential humiliation."

"There is, of course, the possibility I'll get shat on again," I tell her. "Hippos like to mark their territory using a helicopter spin motion with their tail while pooping."

Simone is bent over laughing when a nice young man approaches and brings us to the habitat where the hippos live. There is a large pool of water, but the mother is lying in the sun for the time being and looks very distressed.

The young man says something in Spanish and Simone translates. "He said she is taking too long, and the baby is backwards, I think, I don't know the Spanish word for breech."

An older woman is in the pen with the hippo and when Simone asks a question pointing to her he answers. "Ese es la veterinaria."

The woman notices us and walks over. "Hello, you must be Dr. Locke," she says in English and I'm instantly relieved. I am ashamed I don't speak more Spanish and going through a translator makes everything more difficult. "I'm Dr. Flores and this is Manteca," she says gesturing to the laboring hippo mom.

Simone giggles a little. "Aw, her name is Butter?"

I smile and hold my hand out. "Good to meet you, Dr. Flores, you can call me Shel and this is my colleague, Simone."

"Glad you are here, Shel, follow me," she says and I can tell she is a no-nonsense type of person and I appreciate that.

Simone gives me a little wave as I pass by her. "I'll keep the video rolling, Krueger."

"10-4, Pennywise."

Over the next few hours, I help Dr. Flores, "turn" the baby—meaning I stuck my long arm in the hippo while she massaged the mother's belly to help the little one turn around. Once we achieved the turn, we were able to stand by and let nature take its course. The mom, feeling the time was right after we stepped to the side, ambled her way into the pool and stood there until the baby was born.

"Good girl, bonita, Manteca," I shout, as the baby pops its head up to take its first breath. Dr. Flores gasps next to me as Manteca swivels her head towards me— the idiot who just made a ruckus after her glorious birthing—and opens her huge mouth in a yawn. Fun fact about hippos, when they "yawn" and make a laughing sound, that means you should get the fuck out of dodge.

Dr. Flores jumps the fence next to where we are standing and I follow her. "Dr. Locke, is this your first time with hippos?"

I shake my head, "No, I apologize. I've been with lions and tigers too long and they love it when you chat with them. I forgot that hippos do not and I know they are especially territorial when their young are around."

"Surely, if Manteca was not fresh off giving birth, you might have had some real trouble." Her face is serious for a beat and then she bursts into laughter. "Let's get you washed up, Dr. Locke, and I'll buy you a beer."

After I scrub myself head to toe in the zoo's employee locker room shower, I join Simone and Dr. Flores at the café near a pond of flamingos.

"You are looking fresh as a daisy," Simone says handing me a beer.

"You did very well for your first hippo birth." Dr. Flores holds her beer up and I clink mine in cheers.

"I hope you won't think poorly of me if I say I don't want there to be a second?"

"Of course not, hippos are not to be trifled with and Manteca is ornery in the best of times."

We all laugh. "May I ask where Manteca's mate is? Or was it insemination?"

"Fortunately for us, Tostada is located in a different enclosure behind where Manteca and her calf are now. I'm sure he heard her call after you gave her kudos for motherhood, that was a warning call to all nearby hippos. We are lucky there's just the two of them in all of Central America."

"What will you be calling the third?" I ask. "What should you call the child of Butter and Toast?"

"Her name will be Mariposa. It means butterfly in Spanish," Dr. Flores answers.

"Perfect," We raise our bottles in toast yet again for the Butter family.

By the time we make it back on the road, it's after 5 pm and dark. Simone had one more beer than me so I volunteer to drive. Since the zoo is on the northern side of the city, it adds an hour to our drive home.

"I know it shouldn't but why did watching you shoulder deep in a hippo's vagina turn me on?" Simone asks, rhetorically—I imagine she doesn't want a real response since it's a ridiculous question. The whole day has been surreal.

Instead, I go for hopeful. "Maybe, it's just me that turns you on."

The silence in the small cab of the pickup truck is deafening. When I glance over at Simone, she is looking at me, really getting in there like she hasn't studied me closely enough. Her hand drifts unconsciously to the button at her cleavage and it pops open revealing more freckled flesh. Sexual tension takes over the silence and fills every crevice of the truck, like helium in a balloon.

My hand that is resting on the stick shift moves to her thigh. She's wearing a skirt today, in honor of our day in the city, instead of the muck, she said. I gather the fabric in my hand, inching it up her leg. She fidgets, thighs coming together for some friction and relief. As my hand wanders higher, taking the skirt with it, Simone's breathing is almost panting. I brush the back of my fingers over the front of her underwear and feel the dampness there.

"Shel," she pleads as I graze my fingers over her again and her hand grips my wrist. Her hips gently gyrate as her legs open a bit more. Instead of a light touch, this time I press my fingers to where she is directing them with her hand on mine.

"You are so beautiful like this, free and sexy." She licks her lips as I glance at her, then returning my eyes to the road. There's something hot about pleasuring someone while attending to another task. My main focus is making her come as soon as possible, while getting us safely to our destination. Lucky for me, she is happy to help me get her there.

Her breaths are faster now and she's pulled her panties to the side so my fingers feel her hot, wet center. She continues to writhe against my hand, using me as a masturbatory tool. I slide my hand farther down and enter her with one finger, then two, as she pulls my hand back and forth. When I feel her start to tense, I lightly clamp her clit between my index and middle finger.

"Oh, fuck, fuck, fuck," she huffs out and follows those exclamations with a moan. It's the hottest thing I've seen in a long time.

While she comes back to earth, I push her panties back in place and pull her skirt back down. Her eyes are on me the whole time so she gasps when I lick the fingers that were inside her. My hand then goes to my lap where my dick has never been harder and I squeeze myself. I'm looking forward to my shower so I can have my own release.

These thoughts are interrupted by Simone moving my hand and replacing it with her own. She is barely touching me and I'm so close to exploding.

"Jesus, how do walk around with this thing?" she asks running her palm over my length.

"It's not going to take much," I whisper, keeping my eyes on the road. I'm afraid to look at her for fear of coming too soon. Her fingers fumble with my fly and I realize she's going to make flesh to flesh contact with my dick and I shiver in anticipation.

As her hand grips the base of my shaft, I struggle to keep my eyes on the road, wanting desperately to see her delicate fingers on me. What I don't expect is to suddenly feel the wet warmth of her mouth enveloping the crown of my dick, nor am I prepared for her tongue to lick the pre-ejaculate from the tip.

"Oh, Simone, Jesus," I say wanting so badly to close my eyes and lean my head back so I can enjoy the sensations. Choosing to not get us into an accident, I instead focus on the lights lining the dark road, and place my free hand on the back of her head, stroking her silky hair.

If pressed I'll always say that penetrative sex is my favorite part of coupling, but there is a special place for a blow job. The deep connection to another person, and the carnality of being inside another person is what I love most about intercourse. Equality in making love is always my top priority.

Today, though, right at this moment? Nothing else compares. Simone's mouth on me is the end. She continues to squeeze and stroke my shaft, while lightly sucking the tip. Just as I feel like I can't take anymore, she glides her mouth completely over me, taking me deep in her throat. My size has been noted, so there's no way she has taken all of me, but it feels like she is. My hips move with her, as she fucks me with her mouth. I know it should read the other way but it would be inaccurate.

At some point, I can't concentrate on driving so I pull over and engage the emergency brake. Once I do so, I get my wish of being able to throw my head back and enjoy. Simone's hands, mouth and tongue are almost too much on their own but together I'm no match. When I feel her fingers cup my balls and lightly tug on them, I lose all control.

My hand tightens in her hair as my hips move more forcefully with her mouth. Her grip on my testicles tightens and I groan.

"Coming," I huff out, not sure what to expect from her so of course she shocks me by taking me deeper and finishing me off.

I loosen my hold on her hair as she licks me clean, puts my dick back in my pants and does up my fly. We are both breathing heavily in our post orgasmic haze and are happy to just sit with each other.

After a few minutes, she turns to me. "We should probably get going, even after that mouthful I'm starving." She gestures to my lap and we both laugh.

CHAPTER 12

GET READY TO FLY

WOMEN ARE NOT to be trifled with. Please don't be mad that I just compared them to hippos—you know what I mean. When Simone and I return from our adventure-filled day, we are greeted as heroes and fed the most delicious vegan feast of peanut soup, kale salad, and of course, rice and beans with avocados we bought at the market.

"Nigel cooked tonight, and made his famous soup just for you, bringer of hippo life." Nancy raises my hands over my head as she says this last phrase.

"I'm, not sure if I'd go so far, but I'm glad I was able to help poor Manteca deliver her calf more safely." I tuck my chin a bit, not used to the attention.

"Is it true you had your entire arm up her girly bits?" Nigel asks and I'm sure my face is a bit flushed as I think instead of my hand on Simone's girly bits.

She sits across from me, devouring her food and gulping another beer. I can see her smile a little when Nigel mentions the bits, but she is different now that we are here. I feel it and I'm not sure I like it because it feels heartbreakingly familiar.

Throughout the meal, Simone is smiling, answering questions, and joking about hippo vaginas. When I try to catch her eye, I'm unsuccessful and my heart sinks. Our drive home from the zoo was a big moment for me, and now I'm thinking it was only me.

After we eat, Simone excuses herself to shower and get ready for bed. I hang back and talk with Nigel about some of the more disgusting animal stories we have. Naturally, mine are mostly weird things you find in a dog's stomach, where his are lion with an abscessed tooth drooling and spraying pus everywhere type tales.

Later, probably too much later, I head to our tent to turn in. I'm not surprised to find Simone snuggled up and snoring away, but am a bit disappointed. Despite her state of consciousness, I drop a kiss to her forehead and retreat to my own cot. Once I'm settled, I realize the tent is quiet.

"Hey, I'm sorry I was weird," Simone whispers. "I had too much beer and too much innuendo for one day."

I roll to my side to face her. "You got scared and I respect that."

"No, Shel, you shouldn't because it's coward's behavior. I don't want to be like your one-night ladies."

"You are decidedly not like them."

Her smile shines in the low light. "That's my hope. Can I tell you a story?"

"You can tell me anything."

"Ugh, why are you so nice to me, when I've been a jerk since we've gotten back to camp?"

"This answer will probably irritate you more, but I'm used to your reaction, I don't like it and it makes me unhappy, but I understand." I think the fact that I do understand when women push me away after sexual encounters makes it even worse that I continue the cycle. It doesn't seem like the time to divulge this information to her so I keep that to myself.

"It does irritate me because you deserve better treatment." I shrug at her and she shakes her head and continues. "After I graduated and moved back home, I met a guy and we were together for four years. It's funny how different we are, Shel, I'm the relationship girl, I've been with only a handful of partners and I've never had a one-night stand."

"The fact that you're a relationship person makes me like you more. I think in my heart I am one too, I just sabotage myself." She nods.

"Jett and I met at a music festival and started dating. After about a year, we got a place together and it seemed like we were on a set path. We were head over heels in love and committed to each other."

"I'm sensing a 'but' coming in this story."

She laughs. "God, you're so weird. Of course, there's a 'but' because we are no longer together."

"I hoped but didn't want to assume."

She gently flips me off. "You actually think I'd mess around with you if I was in a relationship?"

"No, *but* it's not out of the realm of possibility since it's happened to me before."

"Noted. Like I said, Jett and I were living together, on the marriage track and then like some cliché I walk in on him with another man."

"Another," I pause, a little confused, "man?"

"Yes, I came home early from a trip and when I walked in our apartment, he was making love to a young man." She runs her hands through her hair. "When we met, he let me know he was bisexual and I had no issue with it. I still don't. Him being unfaithful was what was hard for me to take—I was in denial for a little bit, thinking it was just him slaking a need. It took a lot of time, therapy, and him admitting to sleeping with other women while we were together to realize it wasn't a me problem."

"Sounds like a Jett problem," I say. "Clearly, it's his loss."

She shrugs again. "He was devastated that I broke it off. When we talked and he admitted to the other women, he thought I'd forgive him. I think that hurt more, that he wouldn't see what he did as a total betrayal to me. It's like he didn't know me at all. It crushed my trust in him and made me question every-thing about our time together. It's made me wary of starting anything serious with someone."

"Are you wary of me?" I ask.

"Yes, and no. Yes, because you've been honest about your past, no because I've decided we aren't serious."

My heart sinks because I know I'm going to go along with whatever she labels this. "You've decided, huh?" I ask, trying to keep things light.

"I have, out of necessity and reality. We will be in close quarters for another few weeks and I'm allowing myself to be casual with you because I like you and am hot for you, sexually."

"Your honesty is refreshing. I am amenable to casual if that's what you're offering."

"It's all I can offer right now," she says stretching her arms overhead, yawning.

"I feel the same way, I'm off the charts exhausted." I wiggle my right hand trying to lighten the mood. "This has been in two vaginas today and that's a record for me."

Simone's jaw drops and for a moment I think I miscalculated my comment but am full of relief when she starts laughing. "I can't believe you just said that, Dr. Sheldon Locke. The nerve."

Our laughter dies down and as our breath evens out and we drift off to sleep. I smile because she's taking a chance on me and I want to win her over, more than anything.

The next two days are chaotic, packed with shopping trips, packing, cage construction, feedings (cats and humans), and vet checks of the animals. If Simone and I thought we'd have any moments to ourselves where we'd feel like fooling around, we were fooling ourselves.

It's the day before we leave and I've spent the morning checking each cat one by one. I'm especially happy to report that Tasha and Kamal have both finally had somewhat solid poops. This bodes well for people having to clean up the inside of a giant airplane after 30 some hours of large mammals urinating and defecating at will. I mean, it's still a disgusting job, but why make it more horrifying by adding projectile diarrhea?

My check in with Quique goes as expected. We do our dance, he lets me get close enough to see he remains a healthy tiger, still ornery, but healthy. It's when I venture to the cage next to his, housing his "wives" and children that he voices his displeasure.

Fabia, one of his mates, appears to be sleeping but on closer inspection, I can see that she's having a seizure. We've been giving her and Gala seizure meds daily but she hasn't gotten her dose yet today. I feel horrible, both because the seizure meds make them a bit stuporous, and that I didn't get her the meds in time to keep her from seizing. When she stops and sits up, I offer her some chopped up meat, with her medication hidden inside.

She ambles over and takes my offering and Quique loses it. In his cage, he paces, growls and paws angrily at me. I try to ignore him, but he is a presence that demands attention.

"Fabia, bonita, you'll be okay, sweet girl," I soothe her and she chuffs at me and takes another bite of the meat I offer her. Turn my head to Quique's cage and he is not calm, still threatening me with his roars and paws. "I guess our short mutual respect friendship is now over, huh? We are okay until I mess with your main special lady—I see how it is."

I notice Simone approaching, trying not to laugh. "What have you done to our tiger king here?" she asks as she gives Quique's cage a wide berth.

"I've dared to help treat his number one wife." I gesture to Fabia, who is licking her paws like there's no drama happening a few feet away.

"Ooh, you should know better than to mess with any of his women."

"If mess with means monitoring her seizure then giving her medication, then I guess you're right, how dare I?" I lean the back of my hand against Fabia's cage and she rubs the top of her head against it. This only serves to piss Quique off more as he rises up on his hind legs and continues to roar his displeasure. "That's the way it's going to be now, huh, Quique? I can handle it."

I finish feeding Fabia and stand on the opposite side of her cage from where the big guy is as he continues to bellow at me, to make sure she's okay. Simone keeps me company.

"Would you get mad if you saw someone messing with your lady like that?"

"Hmm, I'm not particularly territorial or much of a jealous person. In the few relationships I've had, I trusted the woman to be able to take care of herself and know what she was doing. I have no propriety over her."

Simone huffs out a chuckle. "Good to know ownership isn't one of your kinks."

"I think I have enough of those already," I say and give her a wink.

"Stop the presses, are you flirting with me?"

"Why wouldn't I?"

"There's no real reason, it's just not something I've seen you do before." I nod because my flirt game is very weak, according to my friend Paul who could write a dissertation on flirting. "You are atrocious at it if you were wondering."

"I wasn't particularly, but thank you for your honesty, as usual, Ms. Lyon." I move to the next caged-in area to where the three new cubs are and as we approach, they all bound over looking for attention. Luckily for them, they weren't exposed to much abuse, as there wasn't much expected of them yet except to be cute and snuggly. Therefore, they aren't afraid of humans, like the other cats here.

"Look at you cuties, I can't believe we let Nigel name them," she says pointing to the temporary chalked in sign which reads, Moe, Larry, and Curly. "At least the girl is Curly and not Larry."

While I stroke Moe's ears, I check for any issues or anything we may have missed since picking these three up. After scratching all three behind the ears I give them a clean bill of health and head to where Emilio and Gloria are enjoying some togetherness, laying side by side, swatting flies with their tails.

"His lip looks so much better already," Simone comments and I agree. "They are going to be very unhappy to be separated for the flight. Gloria doesn't like him out of her sight. She paced the entire time Emilio was in surgery. Their dedication to each other is inspiring."

"Ms. Lyon, are you a romantic?"

"Only for animals," she says smiling at me.

"Do you consider me an animal?"

"Completely."

CHAPTER 13

GET A LOAD OF THIS

A FEW HOURS before we are set to start loading the lions and tigers, a Mayan priestess comes to bless them and their journey.

"This is stunning," I say as the priestess hands out flowers and candles for us to bond with the land and the animals. In the middle of the yard where all the cats are located, we light hundreds of candles and make promises to take care of them.

The priestess blesses each animal by name as we throw flowers into the wind. It feels elemental and good. Simone, Nancy, and Nigel are in tears the entire ceremony and I well up a few times myself. It's a special thing to feel like you are a part of something bigger than yourself, that is a blessing to the world.

After the ceremony, we have about 30 minutes to eat, change our clothes and make sure all our bags were packed and in the cargo van. Nancy says it would be embarrassing to be held up if it was a human who forgot to pack their own items.

We are finishing up our dinner when the camp comes alive with camera clicks and loud voices. "The press is here!" Nancy exclaims, standing and gesturing for everyone to do the same. We file out of the cantina and follow Nancy back to the cat yard.

Not only are there several journalists, cameras, video equipment, there are also important government officials. It's a huge deal for Guatemala to be seen as a safe place for animals, a civilized nation. Or so Nancy tells me.

Simone and I answer some questions about the whole operation and how we rescued the lion cubs recently. We mainly speak with the print journalists while the government officials and Nancy and Nigel are interviewed on camera for the big news. All of the camp employees are dressed for travel, keeping in mind how messy it will be loading 17 lions and tigers into crates and then those crates onto a plane. The officials on the other hand are in head-to-toe bespoke suits, hair coiffed, and make-up done.

"It's a big deal here. People are proud of what's going on," Simone whispers to me as I watch Nigel and a local mayor (I think) shake hands as she smiles up at him.

"They should be, all of this is overwhelming and amazing."

Don't get me wrong, I think being a veterinarian is a noble profession. One of the reasons I wanted to become one was because I felt like I could do some good in the world, on a local level.

"Señor, may we have a word?" A nicely dressed older man approaches me with a younger woman holding a camera.

I stand a little straighter and smile. "Of course."

"Please tell us your name and what you do here," he says while pointing his microphone at me.

"I'm Dr. Sheldon Locke and I'm the house veterinarian. I'm here to make sure the cats are as healthy as they can be."

"Great, doctor, how is the health of the cats?"

"Well, it's mixed but generally good. Unfortunately, many of these lions and tigers have been overbred, malnourished, and abused. My job has been to make sure they are as comfortable as possible especially for the epic plane ride to South Africa."

He looks at Simone who has been standing close to me since he approached. "Who is this beautiful young woman standing next to you?" he asks and I feel Simone stiffen at the 'beautiful' remark.

"I am Simone Lyon and I'm head of PR and marketing for Freedom Roar. Mainly I deal with reporters like yourself, and look for opportunities to promote our rescue to get more support." Her smile is deadly and fake. I take a small step away from her and I feel her grip my elbow. "When here at camp, I jump in and help with all manner of things. Dr. Locke can tell you about a recent exciting rescue we made."

The reporter turns to me very interested. "A rescue?"

I rub the back of my neck which is getting progressively sweatier. Being interviewed is not my idea of fun. Somehow Simone senses it and is having fun at my expense. I level a look at her that says I will exact revenge.

"Yes, Ms. Lyon and I had to negotiate a rescue of a lioness and her cub. There was shouting, a few gunshots and an exchange of quetzals."

"Oh my, that sounds like quite the adventure," he says and Simone pinches my elbow.

"Ms. Lyon kept her wits about her and was able to rescue a baby howler monkey as well. She's a formidable partner when a level head is needed."

"Sounds like you two have become quite a team," the reporter says with a leer and a wink at me. "Thank you for your time,"

He walks away towards where Nancy and Nigel are speaking and I let out a sigh of relief.

"What a sexist asshole," Simone comments and she's not wrong. "Sometimes I forget how old fashioned this country can be."

I turn to her. "You don't think we've become 'quite a team?'" I ask waggling my eyebrows.

"If you'd get over yourself, I'd say maybe."

We give a few more short interviews and pose for about a thousand photos when the press and government officials finally leave.

"Everyone take a break to finish eating or just relax. We will begin loading at midnight so make sure you are ready." Nancy tells us and then waves a hand in dismissal.

After one last meal in the cantina, I head to the tent to get some rest. Simone left before me headed to the main tent to make some last minute calls. She must still be working because the tent is empty and when I say empty, it is empty. All that remains are the two bunks to be stored away after we leave.

I lay down on the unmade cot and take my phone out. This adventure really has been amazing and it's hardly over. I've tried to post on social media as much as possible in order to share with my friends and family. After posting pictures from today, I open my messaging app and send a text to Suzy and Frank. They've never met but we have a three way group text that Frank hates but still participates in. That's just how Suzy is, she attracts everyone, even someone like Frank, who hates people in general.

Me: *Hey kids, just checking in on my last night in Guatemala.*

Frank: *Please don't ever call me "kids" again.*

Suzy: *Could you imagine if Sheldon was our father? It sounds weird but also makes sense?*

Me: *I'm not sure why I decided to text you two.*

Frank: *This is me giving you permission to not text me, ever.*

Suzy: *Aww, FF, then where would I get my ghosting tips from? You have the best ways of peace-ing out of any situation.*

Frank: *Thank you. (Me secretly wishing I could ghost out of the universe or at least this group text.)*

Me: *Don't let me interrupt your anti-social commiseration. Suzy, it's impossible for you to ghost because you light up any room and are instantly missed when you leave.*

Suzy: *I knew I kept you around for reasons.*

Frank: *He's elevated flattery to an art form, it's impressive, and has motivated me to work on my insults.*

Me: *I have a question for you both.*

I interrupt them knowing they could go on for a while with the banter.

Suzy: *OOH-rubs hands together. Is this about the redhead?*

Frank: *I don't give advice.*

Me: *Yes, it is about her, and Frank you lie.*

Suzy: *Ignore FF, he loves that you see him as some wise sage.*

Frank: *I really don't. Please leave me alone.*

Me: *Simone and I have had a few romantic interludes and I really like her.*

Suzy: *So you've fucked her and are in love? We know the story well, Shel.*

Me: *No, we've fooled around a little and have talked a lot but there's been no intercourse yet.*

Frank: *Can I advise that you not use words like intercourse?*

Me: *My dilemma is that I really like her and she wants to keep it casual.*

Suzy: *Tale as old as time....*

Frank: *This is not a new problem for you, Shel, but it is a new situation. You are forced to spend time with her for at least another week or two?*

Me: *Yes, we are staying in South Africa for another two weeks. We will have separate rooms though.*

Suzy: *Bud, just be yourself, spend time with her and don't sleep with her. She'll be gagging for it by the end of the trip.*

Frank: *Such a gentle lady you are, Suzy.*

Suzy: *Several middle finger emojis.*

Frank: *She is right, just be yourself and stop overthinking every little detail. If you are meant to be with her, then it will happen. If not, then you'll accept it and move on.*

Me: *Do you think she might like me too, but is afraid?*

Suzy: *Has she seen your King Kong D? She should be very afraid.*

Me: *She's seen it.*

Frank: *Can we not?*

Frank: *To answer your question, she may be afraid, or she may just want to be casual because she's a busy person. If you are getting along and sharing stories with each other, I'm sure she likes you. Most women don't kiss and fool around with men they don't like.*

Suzy: *HAHAHAHAHA!*

Suzy: *We do that all the time. BUT! It sounds like she enjoys your company and if she's seen the python and didn't run, then she likes you.*

Me: *I don't feel reassured.*

Frank: *That's not what you wanted since you texted us. You wanted the truth. If you wanted reassurance, you would have texted Joe.*

Suzy: *Yep, FF and I keep it real.*

Frank: I have to go, I hear the baby crying. Also, Suzy, the best way to ghost out of any situation is to have a kid. It's an eternal excuse.

Suzy: *Thanks for the biological clock reminder, asshole.*

Me: *Thanks, feeling so supported.*

Frank: *Do you not have Joe's number?*

Suzy: *LOL*

Me: *I'll text you when we get to SA.*

Suzy: *Please do, and be safe!*

Frank: *Enjoy the adventure, man. We are all rooting for you.*

I drop my phone on my chest and really think about things. They are both right, I just need to be myself, do my job, and if Simone doesn't like me that way, then I'll move on. It's not like I don't have practice. This feels different though, I thought I've been in love before, when mostly it's been lust or maybe a need to be loved? My parents are great, but they gave me independence at an early age, maybe too early. The lack of affection in my early years has been something I've chased with all of the women I've been with.

This thing with Simone feels different, though. I need her, not just her touching me, but her company, her conversation, just her.

Simone shakes me awake and I can barely see her because it's now dark out.

"Dr. DNA, time to make the donuts."

I shake my head. "Why do I find that disturbing?"

"Because, we are about to be drenched in piss, shit, and blood?" she asks, pinching my side.

I look at her now, leaning over me, close enough that I could pull her in to me. So I do.

Her lips are warm, as are her hands that cradle my face. The kiss is slow but sweet and it's over before I can deepen it.

"We don't have time for that, Dr. Perv," she says, rubbing her thumb over my lip. "Time to load up the cats."

"I've graduated to just Dr. Perv now?" I ask, gently nibbling on her thumb.

She smiles and kisses me again. It's brief but I feel it and think again about how she must feel some affection for me, even if she wishes us to remain friends. I follow her out from under the net and we leave the tent for the last time.

"Feels a little bittersweet leaving our shared home," I say and she laughs.

"I can't wait until you see the South African complex. You will not miss this place at all once you get a load of the real beds and four sturdy walls."

We walk to the loading area and are met with a huge crane that is spewing a ton of exhaust. Unfortunately, we have to load the cats into their individual crates and then they will be placed on several trucks. The truck loading has to happen simultaneously as the cat loading so hence the polluting crane. Luckily, Nigel hands us some masks to wear if the belching diesel bothers us.

It takes four hours to load the animals into expertly designed transport cages. Each cage has a wood floor with a gutter along the edges in order to collect the voluminous amounts of urine. The urine is captured by a foam pad under the floor and can be changed by an accessible drawer. We have scrapers to push their feces to the edges of the cages as well. Regardless of these features, it will get messy.

Each crate was sprayed with the lavender we had searched high and low for and the cats skipped a meal so they would be hungry enough to be lured into the crates. The cages were connected to each enclosure and we had separated all of the cats earlier in the day. They weren't happy about it, especially Emilio and Gloria.

The doors to the transport cages weigh 50 pounds and Rico and I lifted each one. The cats were mostly docile but some were hangry. Emilio and Gloria are regal in their distaste and both nearly fill the crates. Simone and I spray the crates after the animals have eaten with the lavender oil. We will continue to do so for the whole journey. The tigers go nuts for it and are rubbing, licking, and drooling all over the place. A few of the younger tigers fall asleep and remain so while being hoisted by the crane onto the trucks.

By 4 am we have all 17 cats loaded on four flatbeds ready to go to the airport. I'll never get over the sight of the trucks rumbling down the hill slowly carrying all the cats. Rico and I are driving the cargo van to the airport and are the lead car.

I wave goodbye to the camp that has already changed my life for the better as we pull out of the complex.

CHAPTER 14

BLOODY HELL

THE DRIVE IS long and uneventful and when we arrive at the airfield it is still dark. I'm amazed at the size of the cargo plane we will ride in—it's a massive 787 jet and the open door is massive.

"Hellraiser, come in Hellraiser, this is Pennywise over," the walkie-talkie squawks next to me on the seat. I pick it up because Hellraiser (also known as Rico) is driving.

"Go ahead Pennywise, over," I reply.

"Krueger, pull the van all the way forward, and meet at the first flatbed for cat loading, over." Rico drives as far as we can go and not be clear of the plane. The other trucks pull in and form a line.

A different crane from the one at the camp pulls up behind the first truck and shortly after starts loading the first cat onto the plane. Simone and Nancy are standing by, watching two men hook chains onto Emilio's crate. I sneak a look at him and notice he's a little banged up. I make a note to check him once we are inside.

Once the crane is connected Simone and Nancy start to run in the opposite direction and I am confused until I see a tidal wave of lion urine spill from the crate as it rocks back and forth on the chain. I manage to hop out of the way with a minimal amount of splash-back on my already gross boots.

"Thanks a lot for the warning, ladies," I call to them and they laugh. "It's almost like you enjoy seeing me covered in cat waste."

"I most certainly do," Simone quips. "It's like you're a magnet."

"Dr. Locke, we must find humor in such things when we are to be awake for so many hours." Nancy pats my shoulder.

The loading takes less time than at the camp and I manage not to get any more piss on myself. Once the cats are all on the plane, we help the volunteers move the crates and then strap them in. They were all very hungry still so we made sure they all ate and had some water. We were at the airport at 5 am but by the time we are done, it's almost noon.

After I tend to Emilio's wound, I find our seating area. It is a small area behind the pilots with a thin wall dividing us from the cargo hold. To say we are exhausted is an understatement. I feel like a zombie.

I plop down in a seat next to Simone and sigh. "How long is the first flight?"

"It's only an hour so you may want to hold off on sleeping just yet." She makes a good point.

"Yeah, if I fall asleep, I'm not going to able to wake up in an hour." I stretch my arms overhead and then rub my face. "What should we do to stay awake?" I ask and lean into her a bit.

"Shel, there are people around us," she says pretending to be offended.

"Well, I wasn't suggesting you sit on my face, just a game of cards or maybe chat?"

Simone coughs and leans forward in her seat, laughing. I rub her back until she gets herself together. In the small passenger area, there are about a dozen seats. Nigel and Nancy are sharing their row with a couple who are apparently big donors and are here to help. Simone introduced me to MJ and Joe Hales, letting me know they have funded about half of this trip. They seem nice and were eager to jump in to help.

"Are you going to be okay?" I ask her and she sits up nodding, tears in her eyes, a giant smile on her face.

"I feel a little crazy right now, but yes, I'm fine. If you could keep your dirty thoughts to yourself, I can probably handle sitting next to you for the next thirty some hours." Her smile is wide and a little demented but we are so sleep deprived it's normal.

"I can't make any guarantees, for some reason no

sleep equals inappropriate chatter from me." We both lean back in our seats and I hand her a bag.

"What's this?" she asks as she opens it. "Oh, Shel, you didn't."

I smile as she takes out a few foil packages. "I did." When I went inside the airport to use the restroom, I saw a taco stand and ordered a bunch for us to share.

"This is pure delirium but I think I love you right now." I laugh because she's talking to the taco, not me. "Am I supposed to be sharing these with you?" she asks holding the bag a little too tightly.

"That was the idea. I wasn't expecting you to house ten tacos on your own."

"Oh, I could house, for sure."

The smell of our food must make its way to the other part of the seating area because Nigel turns to us and is trying to make out what we are eating. I'm about to feel terrible because we can't share them because they are filled with cheese, chorizo, and carne asada.

"What you got there, Doctor?" Nigel calls to us. We are about to take off so fortunately, he can't come over to us.

"Tacos, Nigel, I'm sorry to say they had no vegan option." My face is bright red.

"No worries, MJ and Joe here brought us some vegan quesadillas and avocado smoothies. I was about to offer you some, but I see there's no need. Carry on, you two," he says with a jovial wink.

"Shit," I whisper, wiping the sweat from my fore-head. "I feel like an ass."

"Don't, it's everyone for themselves during the flights. We are all so consumed with the cats that we forget to take care of ourselves. If it wasn't for you, we'd be eating vegan cheese, and I can't handle another bite of fake food."

"Have you ever tried to eat vegetarian or vegan?"

"Ugh, I don't mean to disparage them, it's a valid lifestyle. I obviously am mostly vegan on these trips and try to eat less meat when I'm home, but it's never worked for me. I always feel empty and unsatisfied." She finishes off a taco and digs around for another, handing me one too.

"I've tried to be vegetarian, but I end up eating too much dessert because I feel like I haven't had enough food. Fortunately, Beto's cooking always felt like enough. I think I've had my lifetime share of rice and beans, though."

"Well, lucky for you, South African starches are mostly cornmeal, squash, and sweet potatoes. They do an amazing vegan stew at the big house where we will be staying and you don't miss the meat. We will have to go to town and have some boerewors, a super yummy sausage. Sometimes they have rice on the side but I prefer mealie pap, which is a yummy porridge." She sighs, a twinkle in her eyes.

"Are you fantasizing about other food while eating this food?" I tease.

"Shel, if I'm not thinking about what you look like naked, I'm thinking about food." She laughs and rolls her eyes. "Look, you're rubbing off on me, you horn-dog."

"Yummy, horn-dog corn dog. Also, you've seen me naked," I say matter-of-factly, shoving a taco in my mouth.

Her eyes glaze over. "Hmm, yes I have."

The short flight to Guadalajara is uneventful and we remain in our seats the whole time. When we land, several Mexican authorities board the plane and insist on us going to customs to check in. I'm worried as we file into an empty room because we have a small window to feed the animals before the long flight to Belgium.

"Can we please go back to the plane?" I hear Nancy plead with one of the officers. "We need to feed the tigers and lions before we take off. You can come get us when someone is working."

The officer nods and we rush back to the plane to begin the gargantuan chore of getting all of the meat spread out. We separate the meat into three to five pounds per cat into buckets and trays. Each lion and tiger has to be hand fed using the tongs we looked all over Guatemala for.

I walk all the way to the back to start with Tasha. Poor thing doesn't look so peppy. "I feel you, girl, here's some dinner," I call to her, holding the tong through the bars. She walks over and takes the meat. Tigers are decidedly not neat eaters and when Tasha takes the meat it squirts blood everywhere, including my shirt.

By the time I make it to Fabia, I look like I took a literal blood bath. Simone is finishing up feeding Gala and Quique is next.

"Keep me covered," I say to Simone and hope she gets my Holy Grail reference.

"Covered with what?" she says and I'm so happy.

"Too late, there he is!"

"Where? Behind the rabbit?" she asks, pointing to Quique who looks very unamused by us lowly humans.

"It is the rabbit. The most foul, cruel, and bad tempered rabbit you've set eyes on!"

"You tit, I soiled my armor I was so scared," she quotes gesturing to her pants which are covered in blood. We both laugh.

"One rabbit stew, coming up," Nancy says as she passes us with a bucket of meat. "I'll mind the rabbit, you two go wash up."

"Run away, run away," Simone and I say at the same

time and skip away from the cargo hold to the seated area.

We are laughing when a steward runs in yelling, "They need the doctor immediately." He points to me dramatically.

I follow him out to the tarmac where there are several of the officers from before gesturing wildly and shouting at me. The pilot yells at me from the cargo hold where he was helping with the feeding. "Hurry!"

I get in the back of the small car that will take me to the customs office. My hands are covered in blood and I'm trying in vain to keep my shirt from dripping on the car's seat. When we arrive at the customs area, instead of it being empty like before, there are about a hundred passengers waiting to be processed. The officers rush me to the front of the line and I can only imagine what these people are thinking of me.

"License!" the official in front of me demands and I take my wallet out and hand it to them. I'm so flustered I think they mean my driver's license. "No, veteranrio."

"Ah," I respond and retrieve it from a pocket in my wallet.

They take a picture and wave me away. I turn to the officials and they turn and start walking back to the car. I sneak a look at a few of the people and they are horrified by me.

The minute I'm back on the plane the steward closes

the doors and prepares us for takeoff. I barely have enough time to wash my hands and change my shirt.

"That was the weirdest experience," I say as I flop down next to Simone.

"I can't believe they took you like that. You looked like you'd just dismembered a body."

"Exactly, and that customs area that was empty before? It felt like there were hundreds of people in there. They looked at me like I'd just murdered a flight full of people."

"I can see you as one of those hot murderers," Simone says tapping her finger to her lip.

"Like a charming serial killer?" I ask.

"You are odd enough with your miniatures that I'd honestly not be surprised if you turned out to be." I nod and we both settle into our seats.

"I guess this wouldn't be a good time to take out my miniature kit," I say half serious.

"Oh man, then your minis would all be a part of the mile-high club," she says. "How cute would that be?"

"Not as cute as if we joined that club," I say and almost immediately regret it.

Her eyes go wide. "Sir, did you just say that?"

"It was an accident, I swear," I say holding my hands up in surrender. "So is that a no?"

"Dr. Dirty, you are too much. You think I want to have sex with you on a plane filled with lions, tigers, and my dad's best friend?" she asks laughing. "I mean, you, covered in blood, running to catch the plane was kind of sexy in a weird way, but I think that's just the exhaustion talking."

"I'm so tired, I don't know what I'm saying."

Thankfully, we are interrupted by the steward with some much appreciated hot towels, and a menu. Both stewards are very friendly and are obsessed with the animals. They both hail from India where they tell me tigers are worshipped.

After a wonderful gourmet meal, Simone and I recline our seats and promptly pass out.

CHAPTER 15

CRYING LIONS

"DOCTOR, DOCTOR," one of the stewards is shaking me awake. "I think there's something wrong."

I shake off the deep sleep I was enjoying and sit up.

"I hear them crying," he says, pointing to the partition.

"Okay, I'll check, thank you." I find my headlamp and venture back to the cargo hold which is pitch black and a little eerie.

I squeeze through the door, trying not to wake anyone, and proceed carefully through what I know is a precarious route. There are ropes, ties, the wood pallets that the crates are sitting on the floor and I could easily trip. All of the cages are covered with blankets in order to keep the cats calm.

My first stop is to check on Fabia, my most frequent seizure sufferer, then Gala, who had a pretty long episode the day before we left. They don't usually make too much noise but I thought he might have heard them. When I lift the blankets, they are both fast asleep, most likely because they are the most sedated of the group.

The tigers are all fine and asleep, and when I peek in on Emilio and Gloria, they both stare back at me quietly. The cubs as well are all curled up in a lion pile, dead to the world.

I'm stalling because I don't want to check on you know who. Quietly and trying my best not to trip, I make my way to his crate. Lifting up the blanket, I peer in and don't see anything but when I angle my head-lamp in the next thing I see are a giant set of fangs and a huge tongue as mighty Quique lunges at me from the back of his cage. I fall back and catch my boot in ropes, struggling to stay upright.

"No, Quique," I whisper yell back at him, trying to catch my breath. He sneers at me as I drop the blanket back in place.

Once I've got myself together, I turn to go back to the passenger area and I nearly bump into Simone. She looks sexy in the kaftan she changed into to sleep after we ate.

"What's going on?" she asks in a low voice.

"The steward thought he heard crying. I checked and except for Quique scaring the pants off me, everything is fine." She is holding my hand and I lift hers to my chest where my heart is still trying to bust its way out.

"Oh man, he really doesn't like you," she says sliding her hand down the front of my sweats. "Liar, your pants are still on." Her hand grazes my now hardening dick.

A cargo hold full of wild animals, smelling of animal and lavender would not be my first choice as a sexual setting. Somehow, it's fitting. Simone turns me around and we walk to the far wall past the cats, where our luggage is neatly organized and secured, conveniently making a surface.

"Turn your lamp off," she says and I click it off and drop it in my pocket. It's really dark but there's some low light along the sides of the plane so I can just make out her face as I cup her cheek and glide my thumb along her luscious lips.

My other hand explores lower, slowly hiking up the skirt of her dress. It's voluminous and yet easy to work the hem up and I soon discover that she has nothing on underneath the garment. I'm glad I didn't know that she was bare under this, otherwise, I would have had improper thoughts. Thoughts are running wild through me now as my hand cups her ass giving it a squeeze.

Her breaths come faster as my fingers delve down the crack of her ass to where she is warm and wet. I pull her closer to me and take her lips with mine and trapping her hand on my dick between us. The kiss is all teeth, tongues, and need, we know where this is headed.

My hand at her face joins the other on her ass as I massage her there and bring her front to mine.

She makes quick work of my sweat pants pushing them down just under my ass so we are both naked below the waist. I hoist her up and her legs wrap around me, grinding her wet heat along my hardness. Like a miracle, she produces a condom from a pocket in her mystery dress.

"This dress is my favorite," I huff out while she rolls the condom over my dick, Smiling, she guides me to her and then slowly pushes me inside her. From the minute she touched me, we have been frantic and rushed. Once she's fully seated and I can feel the heat of her, it's like time stops. Her ass is on the luggage cube, legs wrapped firmly around my waist, I move a hand from her ass to her throat, lingering there as I watch a symphony of sensations wash over her face.

"Your dick is my favorite right now," she says.

My hand at her throat pulses and then I wrap it around her back for leverage. Holding her still I pull almost all the way out, and then slowly back to the hilt. I continue at this pace until I feel a pinch on my ass cheek. Chuckling I give her a return pinch as I slam into her, picking up the pace.

Her head tilts back giving me full access to her beautiful neck. I taste her there and nibble my way to her ear, pulling on her lobe. Hands that were once around my back fall to the luggage to give her more leverage and a better view. I move my hands to grip her hips as I alternately fuck her and grind into her at an angle where I'm hitting her clit.

We are both panting pretty loudly but trying to stifle our cries so we aren't heard, although the engines are loud enough that no one can hear our bodies slapping together, or Simone's low moan as she begins to convulse around me. I'm close as I lean over her and take her mouth as she comes apart under me. I grind into her with small thrusts, prolonging her orgasm and spurring my own on.

We continue to kiss as our bodies calm down. I can't bring myself to leave her just yet so I kiss every inch of her face tenderly then return to her neck. I like it there, it smells like heaven and tastes like her. When her hands go to my hair, I make my way back to her lips. I can't stop kissing her like I'm an addict. Simone Lyon is my tailor-made drug and I want her in my veins, to drown in her.

She tugs lightly on my hair and I pull back to look at her. "We should get back, I'm sure we've scarred Quique for life."

"I'm okay with that since he almost made me face plant earlier." I gently get up, pulling her with me. I pull off the condom and from her magic dress she hands me a tissue so I can wrap it up. As I'm pulling my sweats up and she rights her dress, Emilio lets out a half yawn, half roar.

My headlamp allows us to head back to our seats without waking anyone, the steward who woke me is fast asleep in his chair. Simone and I settle into our seats and I take her hand under her blanket, still needing the connection. She looks my way and gives a small smile just for me.

Fifteen minutes later as I'm still trying to calm myself down enough to fall back to sleep, the roaring started. Emilio starts the rally and Quique answers. Sometimes they are in unison, sometimes alone. It's a sad music but it's the way they communicate. I smile to myself and catch some movement to my left where Nancy and Nigel are asleep.

Nancy gives me a half awake wink. "Listen to my big boys sing," she whispers so I barely hear her.

There's no other place I'd rather be than on a giant cargo plane filled with lions, tigers, amazing people, and Simone. Listening to the music of these cats fills me with joy and I know they'll be okay.

When we awake in the morning, our captain comes back and invites us to come see the view from the cockpit. Simone and I enter the sizable room and the pilot, who is a kind man from Germany, waves his hands wide.

"Europe!" he exclaims and we are wowed by the beautiful sight of land in the morning sun. "We will land in about an hour. Divit and Pari will get you some coffee and bread and then when we land there will be a more substantial meal before we take off again."

We all change back into our jungle clothes, as Nigel calls them, and enjoy some coffee and the feeling of being a little more rested. The prospect of getting off the plane and walking around is something to look forward to, but when we land and they open the cargo door it's freezing. Simone and I double up on our hoodies and fleece while poor MJ, an LA native, is wrapped in some blankets as she shivers.

A lovely Belgian woman boards the plane and takes our breakfast orders. She offers to let us come to the terminal but instead we close the cargo door and snuggle up back in our seats covered in blankets.

We are treated to warm croissants, eggs, and more coffee and then check on the cats. There are a few employees, including Dirk, and our two stewards that wish to help us fill up water bowls for the cats, in exchange for photos. Nigel allows it because it's just a few and Divit and Pari have been so attentive and helpful.

Once we are fed, the cats taken care of, and the plane refueled, we take off again, this time a nine hour jaunt to Doha, Qatar. When we arrive, it's nighttime but warm and balmy, a welcome change from Belgium.

"This is the part I'm dreading," Nancy says beside me as we watch the Qatar crew prepare to move the crates to a new plane. Our final leg to South Africa. We are viewing everything from the terminal after a hearty dinner.

"I know, but they seem to be already on top of things. Just think, the cats are halfway to their forever home. You and Nigel are heroes and this huge undertaking is going as smoothly as it can."

She pats my cheek. "Don't jinx it, my dear. I'm glad you are with us, you complete our family."

I don't know what to say so I just stand and watch the amazing crew move all of the crates out carefully. Our large plane rolls away and a new one rolls in ready to be loaded. Instead of a crane, the crates are lifted and then rolled on a track into the belly of the plane.

The first crate to load is Quique and as the workers stand by as the crate is lifted, they are showered with a waterfall of sloshing urine.

"Oh my, we should have warned them." Nancy covers her mouth with her hands.

"Too late now," I say, "they are soaked."

Despite a few soakings, the loading goes very smoothly. Qatari officials greet us and escort us to our new plane which is even bigger than the first. The cats are in a roomier area with room to all between the crates without the hazards of the ropes and bindings since they are secured to the tracks a different way.

Our new passenger bay is twice the size and we are happy to have more leg room as everyone has a row of seats to themselves. I peer over the seats to where Simone is relaxing with an in-flight magazine.

"You sure you don't want to share?" I ask leaning down to grab her hand.

"As tempting as that sounds, there's zero chance I'm giving up this full row of decadence." She squeezes my hand. "Thank you."

"For what? Drooling on your shoulder last night?" I rub my thumb along the back of her hand knowing exactly what she's thanking me for.

She gives me a side eye and quickly brings my hand to her mouth and kisses it. "You've made this experience much more fun and I appreciate it."

"I feel the same. Are you ready for another ten or so hours of flying?" I ask.

"Nope, but it's not nearly as hard as it's going to be when we land. Rest up Doctor, you'll need it." She winks, releases my hand and goes back to her magazine.

CHAPTER 16

ALMOST THERE

TRYING to sleep on an airplane is difficult. When you are surrounded by lions and tigers roaring, Nigel snoring, and the woman you are crushing on in the next row, it's nearly impossible. My eyes are as dry as the Sahara, my neck aches, and I can't seem to get comfortable. My mind drifts to the many nights I slept out in the barn when I was a kid. If an animal was sick or expecting babies, I would sleep on a pile of hay in the corner of the barn.

My mother thought it was beautiful of me to be so in tune with the animals and never gave me a hard time about it. I'm sure she had to do extra laundry, and I smelled like a barn animal most days, but she saw how important it was to me.

The smell of 17 large cats definitely smells differently from goats, pigs, and chickens, but the permeation of the smells is the same. We've tried to keep the cages clean, scraping the feces to the sides, the unintentional urine disposal as well as the change in pads every time we land. Alas, there's only so much we can do in the space we have so we have to suffer through the odor.

Since I can't sleep, I decide to check on my tigers with seizures, and the lion cubs. This cargo hold has a lot more light but I still wear my headlamp for more visibility. It's cold and even though their cages are all covered with blankets, I worry about the cats. Zippering up my hoodie, I approach Gala's crate. She and Fabia have been put on the other side of the hold from where Quique's crate is located, so he's not disturbed by his women getting regular checkups.

Both tigers are sleeping soundly so I quickly check on the cubs who have had some motion sickness which has been fun for everyone. They are in a cuddle pile and I don't see any signs of sickness among them. I remove my lamp and head to the back of the large hold and sit in one of the jumper seats there in case of turbulence. It's been a while since I've had any time to myself and it's nice to sit in the white noise of the engine and the snores, chuffs, and growls of the cats and just exist.

I wake to a warm hand on my knee. "Hey, what are you doing in here?" Simone asks, kneeling in front of me, looking sleepy and delicious.

"I was taking a walk because I couldn't sleep, just checking in on my patients." I yawn and stretch my arms over my head. When she sees them coming down towards her for a hug, Simone pops up and steps back. "Okay," I choke out.

"Sorry," she says shrugging her shoulders. "You probably think I'm being an ass."

I stand and step into her space, brushing her hair over her shoulder. "Maybe you are, but it's not an unfamiliar thing for me."

She shakes her head. "Why do you let women treat you so poorly?"

"I have no control over anyone. If I'm treated poorly, I remove myself from the relationship. If you think you are treating me poorly, you are mistaken. You are guarding yourself and gave me no expectations, so I have none." I squeeze her shoulder and drop my hand. "I like being with you, maybe more than you like being with me, but I get that you don't want anything serious."

Her head drops and her hands go to the back of her neck.

"I know you were avoiding me today, and I get why. Did it hurt me? I'll admit it did a little, but I understand, Simone."

She lifts her head and places her hands on my chest. "I think I got ahead of myself in that cargo hold, and now I feel a little out of control."

My hand covers hers and I lift it to place a kiss on her palm. "I'll admit I feel like I'm free falling as well. Could be the lack of sleep, the travel, the tension around getting the cats to South Africa safely that are affecting and heightening our emotions. Let's step back and keep being friends. No more lap shenanigans, or cargo fun." I try to lighten the mood because she seems so sad about being physical with me, and that's not what I want.

"You're right, we need to cool it. Thanks for being so great, Dr. Locke." Ouch. I know I'm in trouble when I miss the silly nicknames.

"At your service, Ms. Lyon," I say with a bow. "I guess I'll have to take my sexual frustration out on my miniatures. They are going to be very adventurous."

Simone smiles and I feel better about everything. Well, not everything, but I'm happy to be back to friends and not all the way back to polite co-workers.

"Oh boy, I've never felt bad for inanimate objects before, but your dirty mind let loose on them is frightening."

"You didn't seem so scared last night," I joke.

It's too dark to see if her cheeks go red, but she slaps my shoulder. "I've seen the monster in your pants, Shel, I was definitely a little scared."

We both laugh and her shoulders drop as tension drains from her body.

"I'm so wound up, I can't believe I fell asleep here." I rub my eyes and they feel like sandpaper.

"Nigel's snoring is legendary," she says. "We can watch a movie together and see if that puts us to sleep."

I nod and follow her back to her row of seats. She

sets up her laptop and silently points to a few options. I stifle a laugh and point to the obvious choice, *Monty Python and the Holy Grail.*

"Okay, but we have to keep it down." She hands me a pair of headphones and puts her own on. I settle back and fumble with the blanket until she grabs it and tucks us both into it. I'm sure she means we need to keep our laughing at the movie to low levels, not fooling around noises. Right?

"You're the one who does all the moaning and squealing," I say taking the flirting route.

She squints her eyes and waves her pointer finger. "This is not the friendly business you were just talking about, Doctor."

"Being this close to you, tucked into a blanket has possibilities, and my mind goes there without my permission."

"You are a very sexual person, and aren't used to rolling back your desires, huh?" she asks and is pretty much on the nose.

"Well, I am very much in control of my body and its impulses if that's what you're implying." She shakes her head. "I guess I'm not used to going from sex to friendship because the majority of the women I'm with want nothing to do with me after sex."

"That is a little sad."

I shrug. "Suzy is an exception, but we were friends

first, so it was easy to fall back into it after we decided to stop dating. That was a clear decision, too."

"Yeah, this is all murky, because I still want to climb you like a tree."

"Feeling's mutual," I say and it is.

"What was your first sexual experience like?" She asks.

"I'm not sure I want to tell you," I say. "It's not the best story."

"I'm sorry, Shel, you don't have to tell me anything, especially if it's traumatizing." She takes my hand under the blanket and interlaces her fingers in mine.

I blow out a sigh, and then tell her, because I trust her.

"When I was 14 years old, my days were mostly farm work, school, more farm work, and whatever needed to be done around the compound. I told you my parents were hippies, and although they didn't live on a commune, per se, there were frequent guests on our farm who stayed for months at a time. Sometimes they needed a safe space to get back on their feet, and some-times it was just a visit, but there was always people around and in the summer, there were a lot." I pause, thinking about how much of a party atmosphere it was, and how inappropriate it was for a child and a teen to be around all the free love and free drugs.

"Sounds like fun, but also annoying," Simone comments.

"As a little kid, it was fun because there was always someone willing to play with me or help feed the animals. I was proud of my animals so anyone who was remotely interested had a friend for life."

She laughs. "Not much has changed then?"

"Nope, I was an animal lover from the womb." I don't mention that animals were my only friends for a long time. "One summer, a friend of my mother's parked her camper at the back of one of our fields. They had met at a concert and traveled together. I called her Auntie Rhoda."

Simone's eyes go wide. "Oh boy, I can see where this story is going."

I nod and release my hand from hers and wipe it on my pants. This memory makes my palms sweat. "I spent the summer growing out of all of my clothes faster than my mom could sew me new ones. She had to go to the store and buy me jeans and shirts. This was a fail for her because she made all of our clothes but she couldn't make them fast enough."

"That's amazing," Simone says, "I wish I had a skill like that."

"She still makes me clothes all the time. I could have her make you a dress or a skirt. She has an Etsy shop."

"Yes, yes, stop stalling, Sheldon, get to the deflowering."

I laugh. "By the end of the summer, I was about six

feet tall and was a gangly mess of limbs. Because of all the hard labor I'd been doing, I also had some muscle tone and a pretty nice tan. My mom said I looked like a handsome baby deer. Rhoda and I had a few interactions usually with one of my parents around but nothing out of the ordinary. One night, I was in the barn putting the animals in their pens for bedtime and she came up behind me and hugged me." I shrug. "I wasn't startled or scared because everyone my parents knew was touchy feely and it was normal to me. She asked me what I was doing and I said putting the goats to bed and she asked if I could put her to bed. I agreed, she took my hand, and walked me to her camper."

"You thought she wanted you to tuck her in?" Simone asks giving me a look of disbelief.

I bite on my lower lip and nod. "I didn't understand sexual innuendo because most of the people around me didn't use it. They just talked openly about having sex and all of the details that went with it. There wasn't much I didn't know about sex, I just hadn't had it yet. So when she asked to be tucked in, that's what I thought she wanted. In retrospect, it's a weird request but there was a lot weirder stuff happening on the farm."

"That makes sense. Did she force herself on you?"

"No, but I was not really old enough to consent to anything sexual. When we got to her camper, she whipped her dress off. I'd been taught sex wasn't a big deal so I went along for the ride, I definitely wanted to have sex with her but I was 14 and a walking erection. I would have had sex with anyone offering. For years, I looked at it like a normal sexual experience until at 18 I confessed to my mother and she lost her mind. She had been very frank about consent and talked to me about how to make sure my partner was enthusiastic about what we were doing. It didn't occur to me that I was taken advantage of until I understood what consent meant, and that's why I confessed to my mom about it." After I told my mom, I overheard her yelling on the phone to Rhoda, crying that she hurt her son and that she was dead to her.

"Wow, what a betrayal."

"Yeah, my mom carries a lot of guilt about it. I think that experience along with my upbringing shaped my sexual life into something not as healthy as I'd like it to be. Frank says I'm too giving of myself and use sex to force intimacy when I connect with someone."

"Frank sounds very wise," Simone says and I nod.

"He's the smartest person I know, also the grumpiest."

"Sounds like my kind of person," she says and takes my hand back.

"You're not grumpy," I mention, "neither am I."

"It's all about balance, Dr. DNA," she says. "We can't all be perfect all of the time."

"I'm far from perfect," I say, a little insulted.

"Oh, I am realizing that more each day, but if forced to describe my perfect man, you come pretty close."

"That's the nicest thing anyone has said to me while not having sex."

She smiles and all I want to be is the perfect man for her and only her.

"That doesn't surprise me, knowing how amazing you are at sex."

"It was amazing, huh?" I tease.

She rolls her eyes. "Please, you made me come faster than when I get myself off. That dick of yours should be in the Guinness book of fucking."

"I don't think that's an actual thing," I say loving this conversation.

"It should be and you should be on the first page."

"I aim to please in every sexual encounter, that shouldn't be some anomaly to be rewarded. All people should want to give the most pleasure they can to a partner."

"Stop it," she scolds but still smiling.

"Stop what?"

"If we are going to pause shenanigans then you can't say perfect shit like that."

"I can't help it, maybe we should un-pause?" I ask grazing the back of my hand along her thigh.

She turns back to the laptop that has shut down by now because we've been talking so long. "The only thing I'm un-pausing tonight is this movie."

CHAPTER 17

SOUTH AFRICA, MY TUISTE

WHEN WE FINALLY LAND IN Johannesburg, South Africa, everyone in our group cheers. Simone, Nigel, Nancy, MJ, Joe and I all share a champagne toast as the plane taxis to where we will unload the cats. There is still a four hour drive ahead of us but having the flight part over is a huge relief.

"Cheers to Nigel and Nancy for fighting for and winning freedom for these animals," MJ shouts as we raise our glasses.

"Cheers to Simone for keeping us in line," Nancy toasts.

"Cheers to Shel for staying with us even after being covered in every form of tiger shit, lion piss, and hippo after birth known to man," Nigel says and we all laugh.

"Cheers to MJ and Joe for being rich!" Simone shouts and MJ laughs the loudest.

"Cheers to all of you for giving me the best and most amazing adventure of my life," I say staring at Simone a little drunk, a lot exhausted.

We are whisked through customs, fortunately, and able to change clothes before we exit the terminal. There will be a ton of press, including television so we try to make ourselves as presentable as 40 some hours of travel will allow. At least I'm not covered in blood.

Once we exit the customs terminal, we are mobbed by journalists from all over the world. Nigel, Nancy, MJ and Joe are all interviews by CNN, the BBC, AP, and Simone and I are mostly in the background.

A man in a cowboy hat and boots approaches us. "Can I interview you two?" he asks with a heavy accent I can't place, and we nod.

He asks us a bunch of questions about the logistics and Simone answers most of these.

"Which tiger is the fiercest?" he asks, obviously very interested in the answer.

"Quique," I say without hesitation. "He's the largest of the cats and definitely the most formidable."

"He is and definitely is not a fan of the good doctor here," Simone adds.

"Oh, why is that?" he presses her.

"Quique thinks himself the king of all he surveys, and Dr. Locke is a threat to that kingdom. Initially, there was respect, but Quique's female tiger companions suffer from seizures so the good doctor has had to treat them and touch them far too much for Quique's comfort. He doesn't understand that we're helping them because he's never experienced helpful humans. I can't wait to see him released into his new home, he deserves a peaceful life with his family."

"Thank you," he says and turns away.

"Excuse me, what publication are you from?" I ask.

"China News," he answers before walking into the crowd.

I turn to Simone. "We are going to be on the news in China. How cool is that?"

She smiles and pats my chest. "The coolest, Dr. Mini."

Another man approaches us and I brace myself for more questions but when he holds his hand out, he introduces himself, "Hello, mate, I'm Dr. Bridewell," he says then turns to Simone and kisses her hand. "Ms. Lyon, great to see you again."

I know this man, he's a carnivore specialist veterinarian and has sent me several emails that were borderline micro-managing. He's the resident expert veterinarian in Freedom Roar, and usually is the vet on site (he mentioned this about 100 times), but was unable to come to Guatemala because he was studying cheetahs in Namibia (also mentioned a lot). I was expecting to meet him on this trip but I didn't realize he was meeting us at the airport.

"Dr. Bridewell, a pleasure to meet you in person

finally. So nice of you to meet us here at the airport," I say as he still holds on to Simone's hand. He's in his 40s, I think. He looks good for his age. He's almost as tall as me, and has dark hair pulled back into a small man bun at the nape of his neck. His outfit looks like a costume you'd purchase if you wanted to dress up as a safari adventurer—tan shorts, tan shirt with army green vest, binoculars around his neck, and I shit you not, a giant whip attached to his belt, Indiana Jones style. The only thing missing is the pith helmet and monocle.

"Why of course, dear boy, had to check on my cats, didn't I?" he uses his free hand to pat me on the back and I do not like this person at all.

"Of course, we just made sure they were all set for travel before we deplaned," Simone says and he drops her hand and waves her off.

"Sure you did, I arrived shortly after and double checked. Poor Emilio and his head wound, and Quique is looking quite underfed if you ask me." I bristle because he's clearly insulting our care of the cats.

"Unfortunately, Emilio suffered a few cuts during loading in Guatemala, trust me it looks much better than it did two days ago," I say in my defense.

"Dr. Bridewell, you should have seen the PVC plunger that Dr. Locke made so he could safely clean the wounds. He's very clever." I take a deep breath as Simone defends me as well, her hand rests on my back in support.

"I will be the judge of that. Once we are at the sanctuary, I'll be able to treat him myself." He looks around ready to dismiss us and move on to something better, I'm sure.

"Dr. Locke has gone above and beyond with our tigers and lions, he's been a huge asset to the operation," Simone says and he turns to her, noticing her arm on me, his eyes narrowing.

"It is very unprofessional to fraternize with the help, Ms. Lyon. I thought you were more discerning and professional than that," he says and I step in from of her, feeling her ready to pounce on him like Quique wants to pounce on me.

"Sir, I think you're the one out of line here and maybe you should go say hello to Nigel and Nancy."

He shrugs and shakes his head, mumbling about unprofessional children. I continue to hold Simone back as he saunters his way over to where Nancy and MJ are enjoying some lemonade after being interviewed for over an hour.

"I fucking hate that guy. He's one of Nigel's friends from school and despite his assholery, he really is the top expert in his field. He also works for free, so it's nearly impossible to get rid of him." She takes a lemonade from one of the nice airport staff and he hands me one as well. It's stifling hot in the small room and I'm looking forward to some fresh air. "He hits on me every time I see him so he can stick his fraternizing up his ass."

Secretly, I feel relief that Simone hasn't been with him, the spear of jealousy that went through me when he kissed her hand still fresh.

"Do you want to go outside for a minute?" I ask, gesturing to the door leading to a small courtyard.

She nods and we go out the door. Immediately, I pull her to the side and pin her against the wall where no one can see us from the door. Her surprise turns to a smile and I lean in to kiss her cheek. After our talk last night, we ended up not watching the movie and I went back to my row and stretched out. I slept for the rest of the flight and I assume she did as well. We both look only half like death warmed over instead of whole death like yesterday. Before drifting off, I decided to try to woo her, slowly. Not my usual route, and we have already had sex, so a little backwards, but I'm going to try.

"You are incredibly beautiful when you're homicidal," I say and kiss her other cheek.

She smiles, tugging on my shirt pulling me in for a light kiss on the lips. I back away, grabbing her hand and leading her to sit on a conveniently located bench.

"You say the nicest things," she says as we sit.

"I don't want to be friends," I blurt out before I lose my nerve.

She huffs out a laugh. "Enemies it is!"

I shake my head as we sit smiling at each other. "No, I want to be more than friends, Ms. Lyon."

"Hmm, I can be open to that line of thinking but I need more information."

"I won't pressure you, or have any expectations if you'll let me woo you a little." I hold my thumb and pointer together to show how little.

"I've never been wooed before, doctor, I'm intrigued—especially considering our circumstances."

"I know it's going to be interesting, working together in an environment surrounded by other people all the time, but I think I can make it work." I have some ideas and from what Nancy has told me about the place, there is quite a lot of room to wander and get lost.

"It's only two weeks so it's going to have to be some quality woo."

"I think I can rise to the challenge."

The door swings open and Nigel points to us. "Come on you two, Shel, you're with me and Bridey, Simone you're with Nancy." He turns back to where he came from and we follow.

"Ugh, I'm sorry, Shel, four hours with Dr. Bridewell is torture," she says, squeezing my arm.

I shrug. "Maybe, he's never been in a truck with me before though."

She laughs and it's magical music. "I thought the bracelets were working," she says, pointing to my wrists where I have motion sickness acupressure bands.

I wiggle my hands. "They did in the van to the airport, but who knows when put to the test with a flatbed."

Simone laughs and I feel it in my gut. This woman is special and I'm going to make it work somehow, despite her trust issues and my clinginess.

The slow convoy of trucks winds through South African wilderness that most tourists never see. I'm happily distracted by the beauty outside of my window so my carsickness is forgotten and the droning on about Bridey's accomplishments can be ignored. The cab of the truck is bigger than the ones in Guatemala but still not great for someone as tall as me. I'm folded up in the back seat which is a small bench with about a foot of space between seats. Fortunately for me, the back window is open and I have a pretty good view.

We have four crates on our truck and all of the lions. The way they were loaded allows me to see through a small gap to the side road. I think the thing that sticks out the most is the trees. That and I didn't realize how mountainous it was here. In my mind, I pictured desert plains, not grassy hills. It's beautiful, regardless of my expectations and I'm ecstatic to be here.

"First time in an African country?" Mr. Bridewell asks me.

"Yes, I've always wanted to visit but this is my first opportunity." I love to travel, but my budget never allows the type of trip I want to take to somewhere like South Africa or Botswana. "My hope is to take a research trip one day."

He shakes his head. "You missed out on the best time to go, right after vet school, that's when you have the energy and aren't ruined by all those dogs and cats."

"I guess so," I say wanting this conversation to be over. "It wasn't in the cards for me. After vet school, I worked at two zoos, then helped my parents with their farm. Now that I have my own clinic, I'll have more freedom to travel like I am now."

"Ah, a farm boy, I see the appeal then," he says cryptically.

"Who am I appealing to?" I ask and I'm probably being a bit rude, but I'm kind of over this guy. "I know Nigel here is a fan."

"Number one fan, mate."

"Meant the lovely, Ms. Lyon. Seems like she has you wrapped around her pretty little finger," he says and any shred of respect I had left over for him disappears.

"Ms. Lyon is a brilliant and kind person, I respect her and her work. I'm not wrapped around anyone's finger." I stare out the window willing myself to stay calm.

"Well, you're clearly ignoring Nancy's fraternization rules."

"Bridey, careful mate," Nigel warns. "Simone and Shel have been working very well together for the past few weeks and are professionals."

"Ah, you know I'm taking the piss," he says turning to me and winking. "I've been trying to get Simone to go out for a drink for ages but she always shoots me down."

"Maybe take no for an answer, then?" I ask.

"Oh, you geezer, she's way too young for you and way too nice," Nigel says and although he sounds jovial, there's a warning there.

"All right, all right," Dr. Bridewell says holding his hands up. "I'll leave you both alone. Now, tell me more about these cubs." I know he's not asking me so I go back to ignoring them and enjoying the view. People like Dr. Bridewell always confuse me. I don't understand the entitlement and condescension because I've never felt those things.

I must fall asleep because I wake to Nigel howling like a wolf. Sitting up and rubbing my eyes, I see we've just come over a ridge and the sight before us is stunning. The Freedom Roar Rescue sanctuary is huge and has a minimum of three acres per animal group. The sun is going down making the 100s of acres glow like they are on fire. The feeling is indescribable. Getting these cats to a place where they can peacefully live out their lives is important. It's the least we can do after the years of abuse they suffered.

Nigel continues to howl and the lions in the back answer him. The roars echo through the valley and bring tears to my eyes.

CHAPTER 18

HOT WELCOME

WHEN WE DRIVE through the gates, we are welcomed by a line of workers cheering on our parade of trucks, running alongside them. The trucks pull into a large barn where the animals will spend at least a night or two before we release them.

"Shel, these workers are Zulu and Afrikaners and speak a little English—I can't wait for you to meet them, they're all so lovely," Nancy says to me as we meet in the center of the barn. "We'll have to wait until they finish though."

The minute the trucks turn off, the workers get to it, unloading the crates down ramps and lining them up so we can transition them to their new homes. Simone stands next to me and we watch as the trucks are quickly emptied and all of our cats are finally done with long travel, home at last.

"I've had chills since we crested that hill," Simone says and I nod. "It never gets old delivering these beauties to freedom."

"Do you think we'll be able to release any tonight?" I ask, pointing to the sky looking like it's about to storm.

"I think we'll be able to get a few, but not everyone. You and Bridey will work from the outside in, checking for any obvious injuries or illness and then once approved we can release them one at a time," she says. "Obviously, these people need some footage so hopes are high we can let some loose tonight."

Once all cats are out and lined up, we remove the blankets gently and examine them. My first two charges are Kamal and Tasha, who have fully recovered from their gastro-intestinal issues and are the healthiest of the tigers. Tasha chuffs at me as I offer her a ball of meat from a bucket one of the workers handed me.

"Bonita, Tasha, welcome to your new home," I whisper and she nudges my hand in thanks.

Kamal is a little more wary after forty plus hours of being transported halfway around the world. He slowly leans forward and takes the meat from my hand. Grumbling, he turns his back to me and sits.

"Gracias, Kamal, I appreciate you not aiming at me today," I say and Simone laughs next to me.

"Ah, memories," she jokes. "These two are up first. They are the healthiest off the plane and ready to go. So ready, sweet Tash," Simone coos as Tasha rubs her back on the crate, chuffing loudly. The bottles of lavender spray are wielded by Simone and Nancy and they are spraying the crates to soothe the tigers.

We roll out Kamal and Tasha on forklifts out to their enclosure, the closest to the barn and the lodge. It's drizzling rain but our spirits are up and nothing will bring us down. There are a few cameras around and Nancy is being interviewed by the AP reporter who chose to drive down in one of the trucks.

The forklift drives the crate right up to the door to the 24-foot fence Nigel told me will be charged with an electric current and monitored by guards at all times. Not because the animals might escape, but to keep out poachers.

"All hail, King Kamal, be free," Nigel calls as a man pulls up the gate to the enclosure and then the crate. His new home has endless high grass, a small lake, and a platform in the middle for the tigers to climb on. There are also various swinging ropes, large barrels, and a small heated house if they are cold or they need it.

Simone and I are riveted as we watch Kamal step tentatively from his travel cage onto grass for the first time in his life. His steps turn into a full run as he patrols the perimeter of the space and then runs to the middle and leaps onto the platform. I can barely breathe.

Beeping alerts us to Tasha being brought to the door and I tear my eyes from the beauty that is a free tiger, to his mate. She is pacing and so ready to get out and be with Kamal. The rain has started to pick up but no one cares.

When her door lifts, Tasha bolts directly to Kamal, no hesitation at all. She heads just past the platform to the small lake and leaps, grabbing a knotted rope in midair, then releasing it and landing in the water. Kamal jumps in and they splash and play like tiny kittens. The unbridled joy bursting from them is infectious and I can't stop smiling.

Simone takes my hand and we smile and laugh in wonder at these cats who've suffered so much. Nigel and Nancy join us and we spend the next half hour experiencing the sensation of freedom by watching two tigers run, pounce, and play without a care in the world.

"What must it be like to be able to do whatever you want after being in a cage for most of your life?" Nancy asks. "Every time we do this, I wonder how they must feel and hope they are at peace now."

"They are, and it's all because of you and Nigel. You gave them that and it's an amazing thing," I say and give Nancy a side hug.

"This is your life's work, and what's more noble than saving the beasts?" Simone adds.

"Right now, in this moment, nothing feels better. It's an enormous gift you've given them when they've known nothing but abuse," I say and feel the moment to my toes. "Now let's get the rest!"

The rain really starts coming down when we move over to where Quique and his family will reside. We manage to get him out first, then the rest of his family before the storm really gets going. Luckily for the tigers, there's shelter for them to keep dry, but they all run and play for a bit before joining Quique on one of the platforms with a roof. Once they are all in a giant tiger pile, Quique lifts his head and roars. Kamal and Tasha join in and there's a chorus of tiger roars accompanied by the thunder and pounding rain.

Their music carries my weary body the short walk to the lodge where I'll be spending the next few weeks. After entering, we all rid ourselves of our muddy shoes, sopping raincoats, and strip as far down as we feel comfortable. Some, like Nancy, Nigel, and Bridey, end up in just underwear and we all gather around the fire to warm up.

The main room of the lodge is enormous, with cathedral ceilings, picture windows, and the hearth in the middle, blazing with fire. It's surrounded by large sofas and chairs all looking welcome, but I'm afraid to sit anywhere because I'm half mud at this point. From some hidden speakers, there's music playing, Led Zeppelin I believe. Nancy starts dancing and Nigel and Bridey join in, Simone gives me a look and we both shrug at the same time and also get our groove on. I'm sure the vision of us all dancing, covered in mud, half-dressed is not the sanest looking sight, but nothing can bring down the feeling of joy and sense of accomplishment we have as a group.

I hold my hand out toward Simone, who is wearing leggings and a sports bra and she takes it. Pulling her in, she huffs out a yell in surprise as I bring her to my bare chest. I left my pants on but my shirt was so wet it was dripping everywhere so I ditched it. We rock together in the sensual rhythm of the music.

"You are so beautiful," I whisper in her ear, holding her a little closer.

"I haven't showered in three days, I'm covered in mud and probably some tiger urine, and I feel like an entire sock has been shoved in my mouth," she says laughing her voice a raspy shiver down my spine.

"I said what I said," I respond and then dip her, stealing a quick kiss to her collar bone.

We continue to celebrate for a few songs and then we all retire to our separate rooms to bathe and rest before dinner. My room is on the third floor with Simone next to me. She winks at me before she lets her door click closed.

The room is enormous compared to every space I've slept in the past month. It's all dark wood and rustic, fitting in with the theme of the lodge. I drop my bags and walk to the large window facing outside. Below me I can see Kamal and Tasha rolling in the grass, not caring about the rain at all. It's hard to describe how happy it makes me to be able to witness their joy. To say that the last 48 hours have been a trial is an understatement. I'm so tired I can't feel my skin.

After a very thorough shower, I dress in my last clean outfit, jeans and a Freedom Roar polo shirt. I find a laundry bag and put my very soaked garments in it to be laundered. I wish them good luck, maybe I should just request they burn them and buy new.

I hear a light knock as I'm squinting out the window trying to see where the tigers went. When I turn, I notice a door next to the dresser I was too tired to see when I walked in. The knock comes again and when I open it Simone is standing there looking radiant in her matching polo shirt and jeans. She steps into my personal space, lifts up on her toes and gives me a quick kiss.

"Hi," she says lowering to flat feet.

"Hi," I parrot because I literally can't think of anything else to say.

She laughs as she leads me out of the room. "We are all hot messes right now. Let's try not to fall asleep at the table."

When we arrive in the dining room, there's a few round tables set and a large buffet table loaded down with all types of fruit, bread, and covered pans. We fill up our plates and settle at one of the tables, the only two present.

"Guess everyone else is napping first," she says. "I know if I fall asleep now, I'll be out for a full 24 hours. This way I won't be completely starving when I wake up."

She pops a piece of pineapple in her mouth and moans. "Same, I'm pretty sure I'm tasting color at this point." The food is so good and I'm not even able to appreciate it in my state.

"Everything tastes better in South Africa. I don't know why, but it's true."

"Even vegan food?"

"Yes, somehow."

We continue to eat in silence until I can barely keep my head up. "I have to go lie down or I'll just curl up on the carpet here."

Simone laughs but nods. "Yes, I don't think I'll make it back up without your help."

"We will have to lean on each other."

When we finally make it to our rooms, Simone walks into mine and then through the connecting door, leaving it open. I raise an eyebrow and she shrugs.

"I'm used to sleeping near you," she says whipping her shirt over her head. I stand at the door watching her put one of those kaftans on, then brushing her teeth. I'm mesmerized but I'm also too tired to move. Before she drops into her bed, she comes to me, kisses my chin and gives me a little push.

"Thanks," I say smiling. She takes my place at the

door and watches me strip to my boxers, brush my teeth and meet her back at the door, dipping down to kiss her peach of a mouth.

"I need help," she says. "Let's push off each other so I can make it to my bed."

"Or I can carry you to mine," I say hitching my thumb behind me.

She lays her hand flat on my bare chest and laughs. "I don't have enough energy to make a funny remark about that."

I take her hand, press our palms together, and push. We both spin, giggling while we stumble to our beds.

"Night, Shel," Simone slurs.

"Night," I say and slip into a deep sleep.

CHAPTER 19

RELEASE THE KRAKEN

SOMETHING SOFT DRAGS across my face and I open my eyes, thankful it's Simone leaning over me and not some giant spider.

"Good morning, doctor," she whispers and I have no choice but to grab her and roll her onto her back in my bed. "Oof, so frisky."

I smile down at her, holding her hands over her head. Everything feels natural with her, affection, conversation, and just being together. She's still smiling so I lean in and kiss below her ear peppering kisses across her jaw to her lips. I pause there, looking in her eyes for permission. She grants it by kissing me first. Sinking into her on a lazy morning, at least I think it's morning, is about the best thing ever.

"Hi," I say resting my forehead to hers. "I want to ask you what day it is but somehow I don't care."

Her arms go around my neck, her hands in my hair. "It's morning and because the both of us went to bed at like 8 pm we still got about 12 hours of sleep. I feel like I could go another 12 especially when you pull me in here." She pulls me down for another sweet kiss and is not making a good case for getting up.

"Is it still raining?" I ask my lips at her throat I press my erection to her core.

"If only," she says on a sigh pressing her pelvis to mine. "It's overcast but the perfect day to get the rest of the cats out and free."

"Ugh, such a good reason to get out of bed, even with you in here with me." I roll my hips into hers one more time and then sit up, bringing her with me.

"You being able to manhandle me and throw me around like I'm a feather is an underrated thing I like about you." She buries her face in my neck and inhales. "Your smell is a close second."

"I'm sure I've smelled better," I say pulling her closer.

"Nope," she mumbles and I can feel her soft lips on my throat. "Your scent right now is making me want to make bad choices. Like, be late for breakfast and go without coffee."

I laugh and scooch us to the edge of the bed and then stand, she holds on, her legs wrapped around my waist.

"I guess the no coffee thing got you?" she asks laughing as I carry her with me to where my shirt and jeans were thrown on a chair last night.

"Yes, but I'm finding it hard to let you go." She laughs and I walk her back to the bed with my clothes and toss her down following to kiss her again. When I stand, she looks disheveled and glorious, her hair fanning out around her, cheeks flush with pink.

Her eyes glance down to where my obvious interest for her is poking through my boxers. The lure of coffee pales as her lips part and her breathing picks up. She leans up on her elbows and shakes her head.

"Later," she promises, "get dressed so we can check these kitties and give them a taste of a free life."

I nod as I pull my jeans on, tucking my hard dick away for later then lean down to steal one more kiss. "I'm holding you to that." I push up, throw my shirt on and we head out.

After a lot of sleep, most of us are back to our normal states of being. I'm not sure about Dr. Bridewell because his normal state seems to be 100% asshole, but he's been relatively nice to me. We've worked together to get the tigers and lions fed and administer medication to who needs it.

Emilio's head wound has healed nicely and without infection so I'm happy about that. This afternoon we are releasing the rest of the animals into their new forever homes and it's a beautiful day. The night was cool but it's hot and dry now.

The cubs have also fared well after having motion sickness and not eating much on the trip. Fortunately, they slept most of the way and have bounced back after a lot of water and meat balls. When I say meat balls, I mean a snowball size clump of raw rabbit meat. The Zulu workers create the balls which are perfect for tossing over the high fences. The tigers love it and treat it like a game.

I'm hand feeding the cubs when Simone sidles up to me, looking gorgeous with her fiery hair in two braids, her freckles amplified by the hot African sun. She puts her hand out and I offer her the bucket with more meat. We feed the hungry cubs in silence.

"I'm so looking forward to getting these guys out of these cages," she says, scratching one behind the ears.

"Me too, I'm so thankful they are healthy and will have long happy lives here," I say, knowing some of the other cats won't be so lucky. My concerns are mostly for Fabia and Gala. They've improved and will continue to get better with proper diet and vitamin supplements, but their birth defects are permanent and they will no doubt have some issues down the road. At least they will be happy and free to spend their days with Quique and their family.

After feeding and checking every last lion and tiger, they are ready for release. There are more news outlets coming today and I'm happy that others will be able to share in the joy of these cats beginning their lives free of abuse and neglect. Simone and I are still in our semi-day old clothes but it's hard to care about such things even though we will be on camera.

Gloria and Emilio are first and I'm so happy, next to Tasha and Kamal they are my favorite couple. It's the dedication to each other that makes me feel for them. When they are wheeled over, Nancy waves me over.

"You want to do the honors, doctor?" she asks, gesturing to the crate.

I waste no time hopping up on the roof of Gloria's travel crate and when they have the enclosure gate up, I have the thrill of my life in being able to lift a 50-pound door so a beautiful lioness can take her first steps on the grass of her ancestral continent. Gloria saunters regally out, turning her head left to right slowly, surveying her new domain.

Unlike the tigers, she doesn't run and jump. Instead, she roams the perimeter, sniffing grass, and then thoroughly inspects the platform, finally leaping up the two bottom ones to reach the top. She is still as she looks at her new home.

We make way for Emilio's cage and this time Simone is the one who gets to lift the door. It takes a full five minutes for Emilio to poke his head out of the safety of his crate. Then he sees his mate and runs, leaping up to join Gloria, throws his head back and roars. Gloria rubs her head under his chin and they sit there like that for what feels like an hour but is only minutes. I hug Simone from behind and she leans back. There's been an unspoken agreement that we won't be hiding our special friendship.

Nancy beams at us and turns back to Emilio and Gloria. "Love is such a joy to behold." She gestures to the lions but winks back at me. My heart skips a beat because I know I'm halfway in love with Simone but I haven't the first clue of how she feels, other than the physical attraction.

We watch MJ and Joe help with the release of Venus and Mars and the tigers act like the teenagers they are, splashing in the mud, playing with the tire swing. I'm happy they had a day to recover from travel, like me, they suffer from travel sickness and were lethargic for a lot of the journey. Happily, there's no sign of that today as Simone and I fire balls of meat over the fence and they catch them midair.

The lion cubs are last and are released into a small area temporarily so they can continue to get extra care and they can finish building their big enclosure.

Construction started after we rescued them and will be done in a few weeks.

All three cubs stumble out of the crate and run around the yard of the small gated in area. There are bags of hay for them to play with and tear apart, balls to roll around and a few rope swings to grab onto and twirl. That's what the smallest, Curly, is doing now. She has the rope tight in her jaw and is swinging hitting her brothers as she goes. Moe and Larry wait not so patiently for a turn, despite the fact that there are two other ropes.

We spend the rest of the morning throwing meatballs to the cats, basking in the freedom they have to do whatever they want. Still tired but wholly full of love and light, Simone and I head to the lodge for a late lunch.

There's a spread of bread, cheese, and fruit so Simone and I help ourselves and sit at a table. I move my chair as close to hers as I can and she laughs, playfully pushing my shoulder.

"This is a good day," she says, popping a grape into her mouth. "There's so much about this job that is a struggle, you know? Days like today make it all worth it."

"Being a vet is usually so glamorous," I say sarcastically, "but I agree, today is the best." I leaning and kiss her cheek as MJ, Joe, Nigel, Nancy, and Dr. Bridewell walk in.

"Get a room, you two," Bridewell says with a bit of a better tone.

Simone sits up straight, and I almost feel sorry for him, almost.

"Excuse me, Dr. Bridewell?" she says standing and getting in his face a little. "I know you didn't just say something so inappropriate to me and Dr. Locke. I've put up with your snide comments long enough and today is just too good of a day to let you be nasty."

Nancy comes to her side and wraps her arm around Simone's waist. "I'm sure he regrets saying anything, don't you Bridey?"

He doesn't look happy about it but I couldn't care less. "I'm sorry, Ms. Lyon, it won't happen again."

Nancy leads Dr. Bridewell away as Simone sits and moves her chair a little further away from me. It's barely noticeable but I sense the shift and I don't like it. We finish eating in silence and when I get up to go to my room, Simone remains, making patterns with the left-over icing on her plate where there was once a beautiful piece of cake.

When I get to my room, I'm relieved to find a neat pile of my clean laundry. After showering and changing, I stand at the window, spying on my friends, Kamal and Tasha. They are lounging on the top tier of the platform, Tasha sitting up, Kamal curled up next to her.

There's a tapping on my window and I jump when I see a large white bird there in the well. From what I can tell, it looks like a guinea hen and they seem put out by my presence. I step back from the window and this seems to appease the bird.

I hear Simone return, running the shower and then speaking lowly to someone on her phone, most likely. I wait a few minutes once she's quiet and then knock on our shared door. The whoosh of the door opening directs the clean scent of her straight to my senses. The sight of her in the kaftan she was wearing when we had cargo plane sex goes straight to my dick.

"Hey," I say tentatively, "does your room come with a bird as well?" I ask pointing to my window, keeping it light.

She laughs and walks over to where the bird is now tapping on the glass again. Simone taps back and waves.

"Oh, that's Miss Tulip. She's the welcoming committee, alarm clock, and mother hen. Now that she's found you, you have a friend for life." Simone walks to me and takes my hand. "I'm sorry about dinner. I hate feeling like that. Like that asshole has any power over me and the way I feel."

"How do you feel?" I ask not sure if I want an answer.

She shrugs. "I don't know and I think that's okay for now. I like you a lot, Shel, and I want to see what happens with us. I certainly am not going to let some douche canoe like Bridewell keep me from dating you."

"Oh, so we're dating," I say smiling.

"Ugh, that smile is disarming."

"Are you saying it has power over you?"

She pushes me and I pull her to me for a hug.

"I'm sorry, that was a bad joke—but we are dating," I say and she pinches my side.

"I guess we are," she says and I've never smiled wider.

CHAPTER 20

WE'RE GOING TO NEED A BIGGER BOAT

"MONSTER COCKS ARE AT IT AGAIN?" Simone asks sliding her arms around my shoulders. I'm sitting at the desk in my room with all of my miniatures out.

"Yes, I'm trying to figure out what position to do next." I tap my finger on my mouth, thinking.

"Well, I don't see good old-fashioned missionary or reverse cowgirl," Simone comments.

"Two of my favorites," I say offhand, examining one of the first miniatures I made in this series. The lotus position is a personal favorite as well, but really intimate and only really works if you and your partner have a lot of trust and affection.

"That's lotus, right?" Simone asks and I nod.

"Another favorite but the penis has come loose," I say picking them up and wiggling them so it looks like they are performing.

"I hate it when that happens," she says and I feel her laugh in my soul.

She brings a chair in from her room and sits next to me while I work. Last night after a brief kiss, we went to bed separately. I could tell she was waiting for me to invite her to sleep with me, but I am trying to take it slow.

"Where do you get the supplies?" she asks, picking up a couple in the middle of a doggy-style variation.

"There's a hobby shop in San Francisco where I get the polymer and paints and anything they don't have they will order for me or I can find on the internet. I like using the different flesh-toned polymers so I don't have to paint them. It looks better." All of my couples have natural skin tones, except for a few "alien" couples I experimented with and tossed.

"So you just have to paint on facial features, pubes, and nipples?" she asks.

"Yes, and shading in ass cracks and muscle definition when warranted," I reply while using one of my tools to add veins to a penis.

"Good googly moogly, you definitely have an eye for detail." She leans in. "I do like that they are all different body shapes and colors."

"How boring if they were all the same?"

Simone sits with me in silence as I work and she eventually gets up to get a book and we just exist in the same space, me with my weird hobby and her reading.

We spend the rest of the afternoon this way and when it starts getting dark, I put my things away.

"Want to go for a sunset walk?" I ask her, holding my hand out.

"Very much so," she replies and takes my hand.

"It makes me so happy that this place exists," I say as we walk around the back of some of the tiger enclosures. When we spoke with some of the workers, they told us that Quique hadn't been seen today with most of his family. It's not unlike the dominant male to head out on their own.

"Me too, and I can't wait to rescue more and bring them here. We've barely scratched the surface and our home country is the worst culprit."

We round the corner of the very far end of the fence and I see something rustling in the bushes. It could be a tiger, but it also could be a bird.

"Quique," I call. Another rustle and we walk a little closer. "Quique, bonito!"

"Maybe you should cool it, Shel," Simone says, turning to me. My eyes go wide as I see Quique behind her running to us, snarling. She turns in time to see him lunge for us, getting a jolt from the electricity. This doesn't dissuade him as he jumps up and tears down the whole electrical wire and the pole holding it up.

"Oh shit," I say, slowly backing us up and turning the corner so he can't see us.

Simone takes her phone out and calls someone, probably Nigel.

"We need reinforcement in the second enclosure," she says, pausing for the other person to talk. "Yes, Quique saw someone he doesn't like very much and tore down the far side electrical wire."

I shake my head because him not liking me is an understatement.

Simone disconnects her call as we continue to walk quickly back to the lodge. "I don't know what it is about you, Shel, but that tiger is out for your blood."

"I think I'll just watch him with binoculars from now on."

"Good call," she says taking my arm. "Good news is we now know the electrical isn't tiger proof, bad news is it's going to take a few days to fix it."

"So we're gonna need a bigger boat?" I joke with her.

"Yes, captain."

Dinner tonight is a farewell to Dr. Bridewell as he leaves first thing in the morning to go back to Namibia and his cheetahs. He invites me to come visit in a professional capacity and although it sounds like an amazing experience, I probably won't.

We all sit at one of the bigger tables and have a family style vegan feast with a lot of bread, squash, beans, etc. I also get to try mealie pap which is so good I think about licking my plate.

"So, Dr. Locke, do you like your room?" MJ asks. I know they generously donated the money to build the lodge and it's a beautiful space, there's no denying that.

"It's perfect," I say, "I have a built-in alarm clock in my window sill, and my favorite tiger couple right outside my window."

She laughs. "So you've met Miss Tulip?"

"I have, she even finds me out in the barn and follows me around when checking on the cats."

"Aww, that's good luck, Miss Tulip is very discriminating when finding a guest to dote on." MJ pats my hand.

"I feel lucky, for sure," I say because it's true. "What are the plans for the lodge, if you don't mind me asking?"

Joe leans in with a twinkle in his eye. "Now you're in for it."

"What he means is I'm very passionate about this place Nigel and Nancy created and I want to share it with everyone." She wipes her mouth with a napkin and pushes her plate away. "We want this to be a place of teaching. We will invite local school children to stay and observe the animals in a somewhat natural environment. They'll learn about the abuse they suffered, their medical challenges, and how they play."

"Sounds amazing," I say. "I grew up on a farm and learned so much from the animals."

"Oh, a farm boy, I knew I liked you," Joe says waving his finger at me. "I grew up on a potato farm in Idaho. I was in charge of the goats and chickens until I was old enough to help with planting and harvesting."

"How did that lead you to making movies?" I ask. Joe Hales is a pretty well-known movie producer, apparently. Simone filled me in on our benefactors. MJ comes from an old-school rich family that builds bridges or something. Nancy told her that MJ has the type of generational fortune that could never be spent in a lifetime.

Joe laughs. "You mean how could I leave the glamour of farm life for the streets of LA?"

I laugh too, knowing all too well how down and dirty farms are.

"In addition to potato farming, I was also a theater nerd. I was in every production and was fascinated by how it worked. Directing, casting, rehearsal, turning twenty some people from strangers to family in a few months—all of it made me tingle."

MJ laughs. "Oh, I love it when you tingle, Joe."

He kisses her cheek. "You make me tingle the most, my dear."

"Good answer," Simone says and she and Joe high five.

"I ended up going to UCLA for bioengineering," he says chuckling to himself. "After a semester, I dropped out and lucked into a role in a production of *Chicago*. I loved acting but my real passion was building something from the ground up. I did a few more productions with that company and somehow, I had the balls to pitch a show to the board of directors. They loved it and the rest is history I guess, that show was a breakout hit and allowed me enough money to start my own company where I adapted the show into a movie."

"That was Grapefruit Tree, wasn't it?" Simone chimes in.

"It was," he answers nodding. "I wrote that play at my bartending job where our signature drink was a greyhound. Grapefruits were on my mind. Can't stand them now."

"Joe has produced our documentary films about our rescues and the preserve. We are lucky to have someone so dedicated to the animals." Nigel says this with obvious pride and admiration.

"It's the very least I can do," Joe says and I can tell he likes the attention.

"Was the awful birthday scene in the movie based on a real story?" I ask. In the movie, one of the characters has a party in a restaurant where the kitchen explodes and burns down. There's a scene where his cake is annihilated by a fire hose.

"No one has ever asked me that," Joe says.

"I find that hard to believe," I say.

"Most people ask about the grapefruit sex scene, Sheldon—yes it's based on my 15th birthday when one of our small barns burned down and the firefighters accidentally hosed down my party decorations and cake." He laughs.

"When I turned 13, I had mono and my parents felt so badly for me they had a party in the backyard and no one came. It was humiliating but brought to a whole new low when a large man in a gorilla suit strutted into our yard with a handful of balloons and started singing the *Birthday Song* by the Beatles." MJ shares. "To this day, gorillas freak me out and I can't listen to the Beatles without wanting to cry."

"I had a sweet sixteen, and mum and dad rented out a Mexican restaurant and invited over 50 people. Unfortunately, it was the same night as another more popular boy's birthday so literally one person showed up to mine," Simone says. "My dad was so angry he refused to eat with us and went home. My mom, my two brothers, my one friend and I ate as much of the enormous buffet as we could and we took turns hitting my piñata filled with all this cute leather jewelry that I spent hours choosing for girls and boys. I'll never eat flan again. Somehow, it didn't ruin Mexican food for me, but piñatas make me stabby."

She tells the story laughing and smiling so she's clearly not traumatized by it.

"I can't imagine how you must have felt," I say.

"Meh, I didn't want a big party, it wasn't really my style, but my dad was so excited and I think he took it way harder than I did. I felt bad about the money they spent, and the amount of food. We ate fajitas for a week but had to toss some of it. I ended up giving the jewelry out to friends at school who went to the boy's party. I really didn't take it personally."

"God, I would have had a full-blown drama queen fit if it was me," MJ says and we all laugh and agree. "You are the most sensible of all of us so your reaction is reasonable."

Simone smiles and her cheeks go a little pink. It's true though, there's no one more even-keeled and sensible than her.

"Being sensible can be a curse as well. I find it hard to take risks, but I've gotten much better as I've gotten older at letting myself have adventures that aren't planned." Simone takes a long sip of her wine.

"Sensibility can be hard to find in the younger generations. It's a noble trait," Dr. Bridewell chimes in with his usual disdain for anyone younger than him. "If I hadn't been sensible as a lad, I'd never have been able to become a leader in my field."

"Bollocks, Bridey," Nigel says with a hearty laugh. "You were the biggest wanker for years." Still is in my opinion. "Also, you rode your father's coattails into vet school and large mammal specialty."

I can tell that Nigel is just teasing his friend, and normally Dr. Bridewell would probably let it go or laugh it off. His face is the color of a tomato and he's out for blood.

"Well, at least I'm not a prattling mama's boy who lets his wife lead him around by the balls," Bridey retorts and the table goes silent. What was a fun, story-telling dinner turns into something not so fun. All I want to do is grab Simone's hand and run away, but I can't let Dr. Bridewell get away with such nonsense.

"How-," I start to say but Nancy interrupts me by standing and walk around the table to get right up in Bridey's face.

"You are a pompous windbag and I don't like you, never have," she says stabbing her finger into his chest. "The only reason I put up with your utter nonsense is because Nigel thinks you're his friend. I don't think you are if that's what you think about him. A friend would know that he's the most thoughtful, brave, loving, funny, loyal, and sexy person in the room. You are no friend." He rubs his chest where she poked him while she walks out.

Simone and I follow her as well as MJ and Joe, leaving Bridey to face his old friend alone.

CHAPTER 21

TONIGHT'S THE NIGHT

AT THE VERY TOP of the lodge is an observatory. It's a circular room and is lined with windows in order to see all of the surrounding land. The perimeter is lined with chairs and sofas facing the windows and in the middle are a few rows of bookshelves and some tables and chairs. There are also several telescopes of varying strength around the room set up in front of the windows.

I didn't get to see this room until the third day when it was finally clear enough to see anything.

"Is it possible to be in love with a room?" I ask Nancy as she guides me to one of the large windows. "This is amazing, Nancy, what a wonderful place. All of it is so magical but this," I gesture to the room, "this is something else."

"Thank you, Shel, it is the one room I helped design. I want this to be a place of learning and discovery. I want children and adults to come and study large mammals but not at the cost of the animals. They can have an up close interaction in feeding the lions and then come up here and study their habits in a more relaxed atmosphere, for them and the cats."

"There's so much honor in your work," I say. "Most people think only of saving the animal, not of what's next for them."

"I think the fact that I think I can save them all is what runs me. From the first rabbit I saved from cosmetic testing as a college student to these gorgeous cats, I care about each one."

She and I had chatted about animal testing and her many arrests for freeing animals from labs in her teens and twenties.

"A lot of people care but you act," I say because it's true.

"It took a while but I figured out how to help from beginning to end. Nigel and I had our first successful campaign in Bolivia almost twenty years ago. They had dreadful circuses there and the animals were treated even worse than some of what you saw in Guatemala. Together we figured out how to galvanize a community and get them to vote for our cause. Then we were ready to swoop in and enforce the laws, getting those animals out and either into zoos or large farms."

"It's hard enough to get laws passed, it's the rescuing the animals and giving them a quality life that seems impossible. You and Nigel have succeeded there and it's wholly impressive," I say and I mean it. "It's been an honor to work with you both."

"Aw, Shel, we lucked out with you, anytime you want to join us on any mission, you are welcome."

She and I stand side by side just staring out over the acres of green, occasionally getting a glimpse of orange or tan. Words can't express the impact this experience has had on me. Being a part of something like this has me looking for new ways to contribute.

"We are traveling with MJ and Joe to Joburg to see them off tonight," she says with a wink. "May be a good time for a romantic dinner?"

In the past few days, I've tried to do something romantic or unexpected for Simone. Fortunately, I enlisted Nancy and MJ to help. Simone made a comment about being out of her normal hair conditioner and Nancy, MJ and I found some amazing all-natural hair care products at a shop in Winburg. I left them in her shower to find and when I saw her a few hours later I was rewarded with a deep kiss and an ass grab. Joe and I found a crop of wild daisies while hiking one day and made bouquets for all the women. I left Simone's on her bedside table with a miniature Kama sutra of reverse cowgirl.

"I'm already on it," I say since Nigel told me yesterday they were going, I've been planning a special night for Simone. "Chef has agreed to make tacos and open some wine from his sister's vineyard."

"You do know the way to her heart, Shel," she says and I hope she's right. More and more I'm dreading the day I leave because she could easily cut me off.

"I'm going to ask her to meet me in Paris," I say. My plan after leaving South Africa is to spend a few days in Dubai, and then a week in France. Suzy is meeting me in Dubai but I am on my own in Paris.

"I like that, it's a big risk but you'll know where you stand if she decides to join you. Good luck." Nancy pats my shoulder and leaves me there with my hopeful thoughts.

We see MJ and Joe off after lunch and it's bittersweet. They've only been with us for part of the journey but none of it would have happened without them. I'm glad to have met them.

"Come see us in LA anytime, Shel," MJ says kissing my cheek. "Hopefully we can see you before Halloween."

"Halloween?" I ask tilting my head.

"Didn't Simone tell you about our famous Halloween fundraiser?" She asks tsk-ing at Simone and wagging her finger. "It's so fun and everyone dresses up, the costumes are legendary."

"Well, if I can swing it, I'd love to attend."

"It's in San Francisco at the Fairmont Hotel. I've given you plenty of time to put it on your calendar so you have no excuse." MJ waves my excuse away.

"If you insist, I'll be there," I say and this makes her smile and clap.

I shake Joe's hand then they are off. Simone and I stand waving and watching them drive down the long path.

My hand slips into Simone's and I pull her closer to me. "We are alone."

She shifts around to face me and puts her hands around my neck. "How about we try some of those positions you are so fond of making your minis perform?"

My eyebrows rise and in one fast motion, I cup her ass and throw her over my shoulder. I easily climb the stairs with her in my arms and she laughs as I skip a few, holding on to me for dear life. Our doors are open signaling housekeeping has changed our sheets and straightened up. I'm still not used to that but I'm just pretending we are at a hotel.

I enter my room and toss Simone on the bed, then I close my door, travel through to her room, close her door and return. When I do, I find her sitting up unhooking her bra, already having thrown her shirt off.

"Stop doing my job," I say swatting her hands away from unhooking the last bit. I push her to the bed kissing along her chest, throat and chin, my fingers teasing her nipples through the bra.

"Okay," she says, breathless, "get to work, doctor."

Laughing, I pull her shoes and socks off, unbutton her shorts and pull those off as well. I make quick work of my shirt and shorts, kicking my shoes and socks off at the same time. Once we are both only in our underwear, I climb over her and hover, getting a good look at her flushed skin, long legs, and wild hair.

"If I ever complain about this being work, you should throw me out immediately," I say, brushing her hair out of her eyes. Staring into those blue depths makes my heart skip. I touch my lips to hers, savoring the feel of her, knowing we won't be interrupted. The few times we've fooled around since the cargo hold, we've had to hurry or try to be silent since MJ and Joe's room was directly across from ours.

Simone clings to my hair as I kiss down her neck to the tops of her perfect tits. I pull down the cup of her bra and roll my tongue over her hard nipple. She grips my hair a little as I softly bite and suck on her pink peak. With my other hand, I drag the bra all the way down to her stomach then pinch her other pebbled nipple. I unhook the remaining hook and toss the bra away, leaving us bare from the waist up.

"You feel so good like this, skin to skin," I say as I kiss her again. She tastes like mint and something sweet. Our tongues mingle, hands in each other's hair, pushing and pulling like we can't get close enough. She pushes on my shoulder and we turn so she's on top.

The sight of her astride me topless will burn in my memory. Her arms go over her head, gather her hair, then drop letting the cascade of red fall down her back. She arches and barely touching rocks back and forth over my barely covered erection. I can feel the heat of her through our underwear and if she keeps it up this might be over sooner than we want.

My hands still her hips and I grip her panties and slide them down and off with her help. I glide my hands back up her legs, grazing her ass up her spine where I grab a fistful of hair and pull her down again for a kiss. While we kiss, she lifts her hips and helps me get rid of the last piece of clothing between us. Her wet, hot core rests on my dick which is harder than it's ever been.

A shiver runs through me and must be catching as Simone's body mirrors. "As hot as our cargo sex was, it's nice to take my time with you."

Her hands frame my face, mine palming her other cheeks starting to rock her back and forth over the ridge of my erection. "I'm afraid what too much time with you will do to me and my poor pussy."

I smile, picking the pace trying to get her to let go before I plunge in. There's nowhere I'd rather be than engulfed in her wet heat. She gives up on kissing me as she pants, losing control. "You'll find out what I'm going to do with you as soon as you just let it happen," I say grinding her against me, gripping her ass, my fingers alternately dipping into her core, teasing.

"Oh, fuck yes!" she huffs out, her body tensing then releasing as she rolls into her first orgasm of the day. I've got a lot more to give her and this is just the beginning.

A bead of sweat rolls down her nose and drips on my chin. "Better not be worn out yet," I warn flipping her on her back and entering her in one move that I'm pretty impressed I made happen.

"Holy shit, Shel," she says and her eyes roll back into her head. I stay where I am, fully sheathed in her, dying to move. My hands at her hips, I swivel her back and forth so she is moving a little but it's gentle.

"Is something wrong?" I ask teasing her by pulling out a tiny bit and then pushing back in. I rearrange her legs so they are together and resting over my right shoulder. Her eyes pop open and her moan is loud.

"What's this one called?" she barely breathes out.

"It's the mermaid because your legs are together like a tail," I say gently biting her ankle. "I can't go as deep but it puts pressure on your clit and it's a tighter fit making more friction."

I swivel my hips, lifting her legs a little higher so I can get a better angle.

"If I tie your legs together with a scarf or rope it becomes a pirate's plunder."

"Next time," she says with a cheeky smile. "Now I just need you to fuck me, and I don't care how."

Tingles run up and down my body when she says this because the poses are just that, poses. What really matters is us, being together, giving and receiving pleasure. Releasing her legs, they wrap around me as I lean in to suck on one of her breasts, then I start to pound her into the mattress. My hands rest on either side of her head as I slam my cock into her, our bodies making that sexy slapping sound. Her arms go over her head as she finds the headboard to hold onto and give her purchase. She is not a passive participant as she lifts her hips to meet my thrusts. We are frantic, a little sloppy, but when I press my thumb to her clit between us, I'm pretty sure the lions and tigers can hear her wail as she pulses around me.

Again, I take her legs and throw them over my shoulders—one on each this time, bending her like a pretzel, so I can go deeper. She's a perfect fit for me and when I slow down again her eyes glaze over and I know I can push her over the edge again pretty quickly. I pull out of her and lift her hips up so I can taste her.

"Oh my god, are you trying to kill me?" she asks but then slaps her hand on her face and tilts her hips up to meet my mouth. "Ungh," she groans as I lick my thumb and rub it back and forth over her anus while sucking on her clit.

I feel her starting to tense in that delicious way

before she lets everything go, so I drop her from my mouth and flip her on her stomach, pulling her hips up so I can slide back in. My thumb takes its place back at her asshole as I put pressure there but don't breach. She's mumbling something but none of it makes sense as she comes for the third time, her pussy gripping me as I again start fucking her in earnest. I don't last much longer, finally letting my own release go as I drape over her, my strokes slowing, my thumb still pressing.

We lay like that for a little while until I can't hold myself up anymore so I roll and tuck her in, her the little spoon to my big.

"You okay?" I ask, my smile a mile wide.

"Nope," she says and we laugh.

CHAPTER 22

THE CIRCLE OF LIFE

WE SPEND most of the day in my bed and it's glorious. Chef plans to have dinner ready for us around 7 pm and he's agreed to serve it in the observation room.

"We should get up and shower," I say, stretching my arms over my head.

"That seems like a dumb idea," she replies, running her hand over my bare chest.

I look at her and half smile at her relaxed and thoroughly satisfied face.

"If we shower together, it might be fun," I suggest. "Then we can get a little dressed up for dinner."

She leans up on an elbow looking down at me. "Dressed up, huh? What do you have planned, Dr. Miniperv?"

I lean up to kiss her semi-scowling mouth. "None of your business but you won't know if you don't get up,"

I say bouncing up off the bed in one move, strutting my bare ass into the bathroom.

After a thorough and fun scrub down in the shower, I dress in the best pair of jeans I brought with me and the one button-down shirt I have with me. Simone changes in her room so when she meets me at our shared door it's a pleasant surprise.

Her hair is in a loose braid with strands artfully framing her face. I've never seen her wear any makeup because when working with animals you are covered in dirt by the end of the first hour so it would be gone anyway. Whatever she's applied to her face only amplifies her beauty. Her dress is low cut and another kaftan but she's cinched the waist so it's more form fitting.

"Not gonna lie, these dresses are my favorite," I say toying with the tie at her cleavage. "This color green makes you look like a fairy."

She smiles and curtsies. "Thank you, sir," she says. "All hail the comfy, easy access kaftan that packs well."

I bow to her. "Color me a disciple."

"Nancy introduced me to them a few years ago and I've been obsessed ever since. I think I have over twenty of them." She smoothes down her front, pushing her breasts up. "I almost never wear them out anywhere because I hate wearing underwear with them—I mean, that's the whole point of then to begin with—but I always bring plenty on these trips because they are a godsend on the plane trips and they are great for hot weather."

I take her arm and head in the direction of the stairs to the observatory. She's possibly dipped herself in honey because she smells so sweet. "You are a vision but you also smell like dessert."

"Thanks, Shel it's my lotion. Where are we going? I thought we were having dinner."

"We are," I say and when we reach the top of the stairs, she gasps. Earlier, before MJ and Joe left, I had Nancy help me set up a table next to the window looking out over Kamal and Tasha's space. Two candles are there and I drop her arm to light them, before pulling out a chair for her to sit. The lights are low and after dinner I plan to turn them all the way off so we can see more clearly what the tigers are doing.

Sitting across from Simone, on a real date feels like an accomplishment. I know she's been attracted to me from the start, physical attraction is never my problem with women. Most women find me aesthetically pleasing, it's what's inside that's scared them off in the past. I'm too interested, too nice, too sensitive, too weird, too feminine—trust me I've heard everything. Sitting here with her on a real date makes me happy in a way I have a hard time articulating. That she likes me, despite my weird hobbies, my sensitive nature, and my clinginess, means a lot to me.

"What are you thinking about over there, Shel?" she

asks and I like when she calls me Shel. She reverts to Dr. DNA or Dr. Mini-perv when I'm irritating her or she's angry about something. She calls me Shel when we are physical, when we are talking about our lives in a serious way. If she's calling me Shel, it's a good thing.

"I'm thinking about how lucky I am that I'm here with beautiful you, in this beautiful place, with these beautiful animals," I say and she smiles shaking her head.

"You are truly too much," she says.

"Too much what?" I ask, willing to tone down whatever she deems to be too much.

"Well, I mean it in a good way, so take that look off your face," she says leaning to take my hand. "You're too amazing, too generous, too beautiful, too sexy, too smart."

"Hmm, I guess I can't control those things," I mumble with a shrug. "What are you thinking about?"

"I'm strangely content and so happy to be alone with you for a while. You were supposed to be a bit of fun, and now you're more." My heart soars to hear it and I know I need to chill.

"Snuck up on you, didn't I?" Zero chill.

"Yes, you came out of nowhere with your little dirty minis and handsome face. Who knew you covered in tiger shit would make me even more interested in you?" I pour us some wine and she takes a sip. "Since I've met you, you've seemed too good to be true, and yet, you haven't disappointed me once."

I stand and pull her up with me. "Here's hoping I keep piquing your interest." I walk her over to where there's a small table set up with a buffet style metal dish, a small candle lit under to keep the contents warm, a large bowl of guacamole, lettuce, tomato, mango, pineapple, cheese, sour cream, and an array of salsas. I take the lid off the dish and there we find a stack of corn tortillas, grilled chicken and steak.

"Pinch me," Simone says.

"Why?"

"Because this is the taco bar of my dreams," she says and I think a tear runs down her cheek.

"Did tacos just make you cry a little?" I ask with a chuckle.

She turns to me with wide eyes. "Yes, Dr. DNA, tacos made me tear up, thanks to you."

"I asked the chef if he could throw together a little taco bar and I gave him a list, he definitely delivered. I was worried he'd say no to cooking meat, but he seemed happy about it." Nancy said he used to work for a four-star hotel in Cape Town but retired because he hates tourists. He likes working here because he gets to feed all the guards and cat keepers and they are low maintenance.

"Oh yeah, Chef loves it when he can grill a little meat, has a special grill just for it so everything else in the kitchen can remain vegan." She takes a plate and starts filling it up. "I can't believe you got him to do this for you."

I smile. "I won't lie, I had Nancy's help. Also, he might have had a bad cut on his arm that he let me suture."

"Oh my gosh, are you allowed to do that?" she asks staring at me.

"It's not the most ethical thing, but we are in a foreign country, and I used to practice sutures on my mom and dad all the time. You get a lot of cuts on a farm." Sewing up a dog or a cat is a lot harder than a human since they tend to be more wiggly.

After we both have giant piles of food on our plates, we sit down. Conversation flows, Simone eats a way too hot pepper and has to have an emergency piece of plain tortilla, and I have the best night of my life so far.

When we are finished, we bring our plates to the table and I blow out the candle under the hot dish. I promised Chef I'd pack the food back in the large insulated bags he stacked underneath the table. Simone helps me and when we are done, we head to a soft loveseat facing the window. Before I sit, I grab our wine and turn the lights all the way off, snuffing the candles on our dining table too. It is pitch black in the room but for the light coming in from the floodlight outside the lodge yard.

I settle in next to her, our bodies close and hand her

the wine. We touch glasses and sip, not breaking eye contact. Suddenly, the room floods with light as a bolt of lightning streaks across the sky. Simone jumps and spills her wine.

"Holy shit, that was so bright." We both turn our attention to the sky and listen for the thunder that rumbles not long after. Almost immediately, it begins to pour, ruining our view of the animals as they take shelter under the platforms out of sight. It's okay though, because we have a new show to watch.

A few more bolts shoot through the night as the thunder rolls almost constantly. Then it's back to back to back, lightning flashing in the sky. Simone gets up and throws some pillows on the floor.

"Sit, big guy," she commands and I laugh, but I hustle to do what she says and sit on a pillow facing the window. Simone walks in front of me and unties the knot under her breasts, loosening the dress so it hangs shapeless on her. My dick hardens because I think the next thing she will do is take it off.

She doesn't. Instead, she hikes it up and sits astride me. "Hi," she says as she wraps her arms around my neck. "Thank you for dinner," she says as she places kisses along my jaw. My hands sit on my knees, letting her take the lead for now. She runs her nose along my throat and I swallow so hard it's noticeable. "I've never paid much attention to an Adam's apple, but yours is so sexy." She drags her tongue over said apple as I swallow again.

"Thanks," I whisper and she giggles.

"I don't know where to start with you, it's an embarrassment of riches. All at once, I want to climb you like a tree, sit on your face, and have you bend me over the sofa. Then I think, no, I just want to be slow with you and take my time. There's no wrong answer." She cups my face in her hands, caressing my cheek, touching my lips with her thumb, and then running her hands through my hair.

"I am at your service, Simone, but I have an idea you might like," I say moving my hands from my knees to her ass cheeks. "Unbutton my jeans," I say and after she kisses me on the mouth she does. I lift her up and she stands in from of me as I shove my jeans and underwear all the way off, naked from the waist down. She tries to sit again and I stop her, rolling her kaftan up until I'm met with her sweet, bare pussy. Pulling her to me I lick her seam, lightly sucking on her clit.

"Yes," she says as I move my tongue over her a few times, always taking care to pay attention to her clit, her hands pulling on my hair.

She pulls a little harder and I look up to see her blue green eyes smoldering, her hair wild around her flushed face. Slowly she sinks to her knees taking my dick in her hand guiding it inside her. I sigh and rest my forehead to hers out of breath. Her hands go to her dress and she flings it off in one move. I mirror her and get my shirt off as well. I guide her legs around me as we sit in lotus position.

"This is padmasana, or deep lotus," I say moving my hand to her lower back then grinding her against me. "In order to stay connected, we must hold on to each other tightly. It's an intimate position and perfect for slow or tantric sex."

"You sound like a porn narrator," she says nibbling on my ear and bearing down on my dick.

"Should I stop?" I ask, pulling and pushing on her ass, grinding her on my erection.

"Please don't," she whispers, her head falling back. I reach up and remove the hairband from her braid, threading her hair out so it's loose around her shoulders and back. We stay like this, still for a little, kissing and pulling hair, then things quickly push us to the edge, I always stop us when orgasm is close, and she burrows into my neck, marking me with her teeth and tongue.

My one hand slides up her torso between her breasts as I push her back, supporting her with my other arm. In this position, I can move her up and down with her arms around my neck. I also have a good view of where we connect and of her body, which I am happy to worship —the lightning flashing across her, making her an ethereal being in my mortal presence.

"Jesus, Shel," she huffs out and a bead of sweat drips down her chest to land on her nipple. I lean in for a taste and suck and nibble on her breast. Again, I feel her starting to lose control and I pull her in blocking her from moving with my legs. "I'm not going to recover from this," she says, her face red with exertion and heat.

"Then my goal will be achieved," I say rocking back and forth a little creating minute friction. "Giving you so much pleasure that you'll never be able to think of anyone else." I kiss her then, sending her a message, a promise that I'm the one for her, and I'm here for her and her only.

"Put me out of my misery, my sweet sweet misery," she whines as I still her hips once more.

I lower her down on the pillows, flip her onto her stomach and prop a pillow under her pelvis. My legs surround her, I slide back in and start fucking her harder than before, holding her hips. In this position things are tighter and there's more pressure on her clitoris. Slowing down, I give attention to her neck and kiss along her shoulder. I hold her at the hips and spread her ass cheeks so I can kneel back and watch.

"I need you," she pants in frustration as I glide my palm up her spine, threading my hand in her hair, lightly pulling. My arms are in a push up position as I hover over her picking up speed again. Her moans turn to one long "ah" as she pulses around my dick. Quickly, I hoist her hips up and find my own release while extending her orgasm to meet mine.

We collapse in a heap of sated limbs and then I roll

us so she's laying on top of me, her head nestles into my chest.

"I think I need to drink more water or something if I'm going to keep up with you, Dr. DNA."

"I've heard that the more you practice the easier it gets," I say pinching her bottom.

She rolls her eyes as she kisses my chin. "I can't believe I'm saying this but I agree."

CHAPTER 23

TEMPORARY BLISS

ALL OF MY dreams are coming true. In fact, right now I'm having a really great one, I'm in a movie and Simone is my costar and we are sitting on a porch drinking lemonade with our grandchildren. I know, this isn't the type of dream I normally have about her, you dirty people. Maybe now that I've been with her, and it was the best sex of my life, I have new dreams.

"There you two are!" I hear Nancy's voice way too close for comfort.

"Oh shit," Simone whispers next to me—because we are both butt-ass naked under this blanket.

I crack an eyelid open to see Nancy and Nigel, crap, standing over us smiling like lunatics.

"Good morning, my little sex fiends," Nancy says, clapping her hands and I want to die.

"Oh my God, I want to die," Simone echoes my

thoughts and I laugh pulling her closer to me, making sure all of our bits are secure.

"Oh, Moni, I hope it won't embarrass you that Chef was the one who told us where you were." Nigel's voice booms in between his guffaws of laughter. At least they think it's funny, they could be angry and kick us out of the room they designed to teach children, man we are going to hell.

Simone burrows deeper under the blanket hiding her face which I'm sure is a dark shade of red. I smile at them and Nigel gives me a wink.

"Can you give us a minute or two?" I grumble out. "We must have fallen asleep here by accident."

Nancy and Nigel laugh even harder as they walk out. I scramble to find my underwear and jeans, tossing Simone her kaftan. I watch in awe as she stands to put it on. She's glowing, a little red where my stubble rubbed her skin, flushing from either all the sex we had or the fact that we were busted by basically her aunt and uncle they've known her so long.

Once we are all set, I look over to see that Chef has indeed been here because all evidence of our meal is gone.

"Oh my gosh, how did this happen?" Simone asks.

"Well,..." I say smiling, pulling her down to my lap. I kiss the shell of her ear. "First I got your pussy wet, then," she stops me putting her hand over my mouth.

"You're so lucky I like you, Sheldon. I'm never, and

I mean *never,* going to live this down. Nigel will for sure tell my dad and will dine on this story for years. You have no idea." She sighs but doesn't look too upset about it.

I pinch her hip. "Is it really that bad?" I ask and maybe I don't want the answer.

She looks at me, her face close to mine. "Last night was worth any hassle I get today and in the future." Her hands go to my cheeks and she pulls me in for a deep kiss. Every kiss with her transfers a piece of my soul to her. I'd do anything for one.

"Good answer," I agree, kissing her again and although my morning wood went away in the presence of our bosses, it's back with a vengeance now. I press her closer to me and she definitely feels it. "Shower?"

She flushes all over and plants a kiss on my nose. "Race you." She bolts up and out of the room, knowing I can't follow her because of my raging boner. She turns at the top of the steps. "Okay, that wasn't fair," she says glancing at my crotch. "Meet me in five minutes. I'll get the water warm for you."

"Dear Shel, I guess the date went well?" Nigel walks in, helping my deflating efforts.

"It did, I'm sorry you found us that way, we did mean to go back to our rooms. The storm was so beautiful we wanted to watch from up here. The view was spectacular."

"I'm sure it was, old chap." He slaps my shoulder a

little harder than necessary and I guess we are having this conversation. "Nancy has told me to stay out of it, but I've been the godfather to that girl for a long time, and it's only fair that you and I have a chat since her father isn't here."

"I assure you, Nigel, my intentions are honorable and I'm very serious about Simone," I say and it's true, I'm more than serious, I'm in love with her.

"That's good to hear," he says and pauses. "Nancy told me she clued you in on Simone's past heartbreaks?"

"Yes, sir, and Simone and I have had a few chats about her hesitation when it comes to commitment."

"Hmm, so it's really your feelings I have to worry about?" he asks, and yes because I'm already in too deep. If she ultimately rejects me, I'll be devastated.

"Maybe, but I can hold my own," I say, lying out my ass. Now that my dick is calm, I stand and walk to the stairs. "I'm going to go get ready for the day."

He nods and narrows his eyes at me. "You do that, Doctor."

Steam billows out of my bathroom when I enter my room. I strip my clothes off as fast as I can and join Simone in the shower.

"What took you so long?" she asks. "I'm pruning up." She throws her arms around my neck, kissing my chest.

"Just setting Nigel straight on a few things." Her expression is doubtful.

"Was he being a neanderthal?"

"A little but I told him he had nothing to worry about with me. I'll never hurt you," I say and really mean it.

She kisses me and I scoop my hands under her ass lifting her as she wraps her legs around me. "Done incorrectly, I'm sure shower sex could hurt me," she teases me, rubbing her core down the hard shaft of my dick.

"I strive for perfection," I say and show her my shower sex prowess.

We spend the rest of the day feeding the cats, organizing supplies, and my favorite—playing with the lion cubs. One of the workers, Bobby, found that if you spray them with a hose, they try to attack the water. He and I took turns for an hour shooting water at them until they collapsed in a heap, unable to continue.

Lunch was spent with Nigel, Nancy, and Simone, chatting about the new veterinarian who is to arrive today, and about my trip to Dubai. I could tell Simone was not a fan of that part of the conversation. I dread leaving her too, but only because I think she'll change her mind. It's nice to see her disappointment—I think she will miss me.

"After Dubai, is Paris, right Shel?" Nancy asks and

if she thinks she's not being obvious she's wrong. "Such a romantic city, Nigel and I love to go when we need a little reminder of how hot we are for each other." She waggles her eyebrows.

"I'll remind you later, pet." Aaaand now it's weird. To be fair, Simone and I have been playing footsie this whole lunch, and I've imagined her in at least twelve different positions just in the last half hour.

"Your reminder always gets me there," she says and Simone presses her foot to mine. We exchange a look and I nod my head to the door like maybe we should leave.

"Okay," Simone interrupts. "On that note, Shel and I are going to walk the perimeter and then have a rest until Dr. Stevens and his wife get here."

She takes my hand and we walk out, Nigel and Nancy completely ignoring us, as I watch Nancy lick her lips and Nigel pounce on her kissing her neck.

"Faster, walk faster," Simone says pulling on my hand.

We half run out the front door to the path that takes us around the compound, laughing like idiots.

"Couple goals," she says squeezing my hand and my heart races.

"Would you consider us a couple?" I ask, venturing into dangerous territory.

She stops, her hands rest on her hips. "Are we having the talk right now, Dr. DNA?"

"It's as good a time as any, Ms. Lyon," I say. "You know how I feel about us and what I want."

"Do I?" She tilts her head at me. "I know you've been wanting a relationship and failing with other women, lots of other women," she jabs and I wince.

"Hey, I was honest about my past, don't use it against me, it's not fair."

She slides her foot back and forth in the dust. "You're right, that wasn't fair. You've told me what you want generally but just not specifically with me."

"You want me to be clear?" I ask and she nods. "I want to be with you, I want you to meet me in Paris and spend the week just the two of us. When we get back to California, I want sleepovers, dates, and more sex. I want you to wake up in my bed, walk to the coffee shop, get a burrito, and go to the movies."

She steps into my space and puts her arms around my neck. I love that she does that, it's a possessive move, a comfortable move. "That all sounds good," she says hesitating. "I'm not so sure about Paris."

"Of course, just because I want it doesn't mean I'm going to get it. I just want you to be absolutely clear about my intentions. I like you a lot and want to spend time with you and see where this goes." I bend to kiss her lightly then thread my fingers with hers and continue to walk.

"Did you really plan a trip to Paris by yourself?" she asks.

"I did, I guess I'm an optimist and thought I could create some romance for myself. Maybe find a nice French girl since I wasn't having any luck in North America." She shoves my shoulder.

"I'm sure you would do well in France, they like the sensitive ones." I shove her back playfully.

"Please meet me in Paris?" I ask, sweating all of the sudden. "I'll be there for a whole week and you could come for part or all of the time. I don't know your schedule."

"Are you sure you want me to crash your vacation?" she asks and I still haven't convinced her of my feelings, I guess.

"It won't be much of a vacation if I'm missing you the whole time."

She's quiet for a bit as we walk. It's a nice day, not too hot with enough cloud cover that the sun isn't too strong. Of course, we are both coated in sunscreen and Simone has a wide-brimmed hat keeping her freckles in check. So far we haven't seen any of our cat friends on our walk, but Tulip, the guinea hen has been following us like the paparazzi since we left the lodge.

"Do you want to see some of the other lions later?" she asks. In addition to the animals we brought from South America, there are about 30 or so lions from other South American countries and some from South African zoos. I've met only two because they have rashes on their paws, but they were sedated when I treated them and I haven't been over the hill to the other side of the huge area that Freedom Roar owns.

"Yes, I'd love that," I answer.

"We can drive up to the look-out hill and you can get a good view of most of the land and almost all of the animals."

"A look-out huh?" I comment, raising an eyebrow, "Sounds like a good spot for necking."

"Where did you come from, the 1950s?"

"What? Necking is a perfectly acceptable synonym for making out and should be used more often." I throw my arm around her neck and pull her in for a wet kiss to her cheek.

"Whatever, Fonzie, stop slobbering on me," she says.

"You didn't mind when I was slobbering on your pussy in the shower earlier." Her face is bright red as she stops again with those hands on her hips.

"Sheldon Locke, you are a dirty bird." Her mouth is open in shock.

I thread my arms through hers at her hips and pull her close so she can feel me. "This dirty bird is all yours," I say as I grind my dick against her. I've had an erection more times than I can count on this trip. Thank goodness I've been able to relieve some of them with her. Her hand slides to where I most want her attention. She gently squeezes my dick a few times over the front of my shorts.

"This really is my favorite bird," she says and Tulip squawks at her in offense. We laugh. "Aw, Tulip you're my girl."

I bend to take her mouth, pulling her to me, my hands at her lower back, flirting with the waistband of her jeans. Our kiss is slow, a promise for more later, her lips so soft, so inviting, her tongue twisting with mine. It's not a long kiss but it does nothing to calm me down, I try to wiggle my hands down her jeans and they are tight so it's not an easy feat.

"I think I prefer the kaftans, they are the top of my favorite things list." I finally wedge my hands where I want them, cupping her ass, my fingers searching for more.

"Like Oprah's list?" she asks, mocking me.

"Well, there are only a few things on the list, so no, not like hers."

"What, pray tell, else is on this list?" she asks, cooing as I tease her ass crack.

"Red hair, freckles, kaftans, cargo holds, and lightning." Her eyes light up with amusement as I list all my favorite items. Funny, they are all related to her. I could go on so I do. "Blue-green eyes, Monty Python, road head, monkey rescues, and adventurous women." Her hands caress me as I inch my fingers lower.

"My list includes pervy miniatures, enormous men who get car sick, the things you say, and blue eyes that see right through me." Her pressure increases and I'm about to come in my pants in view of tigers and probably one of the guards. "How you know exactly what I need before I can tell you, tacos, and multiple orgasms, which I've only experienced very recently."

Moving her hand I press her to the ridge of my hard-on, pressing my middle finger in her asshole. "I'll give you one now, then two more in the room, will that do?"

"Yeah," she whimpers as I kiss her again as she goes over the edge.

Our walk ends abruptly and I make good on my promise.

CHAPTER 24

TIME IS MY ENEMY.

The next few days fly by and the thought of leaving is making me feel ill. Simone has been affectionate, and we've been inseparable. Her room is now a glorified closet as we sleep (and do other things) in mine. That decision was easy because the one night we tried to sleep in hers, Tulip made it clear that was a bad decision by hooting and hollering until we moved.

Every morning we would have breakfast then check on all the cats we traveled with as well as the lions that have been in residence for a few years. Our routine includes stopping at the lookout point so we can make out a little and then we drive the jeep down to the other lion enclosures. It's nice to see the future that lies ahead for the tigers and lions we brought here. These cats are happy, well-fed, and are enjoying the freedom to do what they want for the rest of their lives.

After checking all the cats, we usually have lunch in the observatory just the two of us. The rest of the afternoons are full of paperwork, calls and emails for Simone, and supply checks, feeding, and following up on any medical issues with Dr. Stevens. He's a young Australian vet who has been hired to be a live onsite to care for all of the lions and tigers. His wife is here too and she seems a little culture shocked but has settled in pretty well.

In the evening we have what Nancy calls our "family dinner," where we all sit at a large round table and share food, stories, and it's an opportunity for Nigel to give Simone and me a hard time for our shenanigans.

After dinner, Simone and I shower together then that usually leads to other activities. We eventually end up back in the observatory, our favorite place. I'm leaving in two days and I'm starting to panic a little. This is the dangerous time for me because it's when I start to get a little clingy and women don't like that.

Simone is draped over me as we lay on one of the couches, enjoying another lightning storm from afar. This one is so far, we don't hear any thunder.

"I don't think I'll ever get tired of this room," she says while her hands thread through my hair absentmindedly.

"I don't think I'll ever get tired of any room that has

you in it," I say, casually stroking my fingers along her spine.

"You really do say the sweetest things, Shel, I feel like a badass most days, and I have no self-esteem issues, but somehow you make me feel even better. Is this what it's like with you all the time?"

I settle my hands on her ass and squeeze. "I think it is, the best person to ask would be Suzy."

"Is she the one and only ex?"

"Yes, but she only ever liked me as a friend and said she got dick drunk and it blinded her true feelings. She is one of my oldest friends and one night we both got too drunk and hooked up. I'll admit I had real feelings and high hopes, but she just wanted a fuck buddy scenario when it came down to it. She said it was too difficult to say goodbye to my King Kong dick so she let it go on longer than she planned," I say. "That's her name for it, not mine."

"I completely get her attachment," Simone says, rolling her hips on my hardening dick.

"It's embarrassing but she had like a ceremony for it, gave him an award and a speech." I laugh remembering Suzy talking to my dick, then giving it a proper goodbye (a blowjob I'm not going to bring up).

"Suzy sounds like a fun person," she says and I can tell she means it and isn't jealous, not sure how I feel about that. Maybe I want her to feel a little possessive of me.

"She's probably the most fun and loudest person I know. I'm looking forward to seeing her in Dubai. We talk and text all the time but it's rare to see her in person. She's a partner in a law firm in New York, so her free time is scarce." When Suzy suggested meeting in Dubai since she had a client there and the trip was long overdue, I was so happy. To be honest, until I met Simone, I've always felt like Suzy was the one that got away, but I'd never admit it to her because I'd never hear the end of it.

"Wow, how long are you in Dubai for?" she asks and this time I hear a little bit of annoyance in her voice.

"Just four days, and then I head to Paris on the 15th."

Simone pushes up, her hands on my shoulders. "You're going to be together on Valentine's Day?" Now she's a little worked up and I like it.

"You don't strike me as the type to care much about that type of holiday," I say, smiling while I give her a teasing pinch on her side. "Are you feeling threatened by sweet little Suzy?"

"Someone who holds an awards ceremony for your amazing dick doesn't sound all that sweet."

"I'd say my dick would disagree," I say and she smacks her hand on my chest, trying to get out of my grip. "He is only interested in one woman though." She stops struggling, her legs straddle mine and she sits up.

"Oh yeah?" she asks and does a wicked roll of her hips.

"So, you think my dick is amazing?" I tease holding her hips, grinding up into her.

Her head goes back, her hair tickling my thighs. "It's fine," she clips out.

"Well, my amazing dick wants in your terrific pussy," I whisper, rolling her back and forth on my shaft. At this point, we are basically having sex with our clothes on. We are alone, it's late-ish and it's dark in here.

She sits up again and lifts herself off me to pull down my sleep pants I changed into after dinner. Once my dick is free, she surprises me by leaning forward and sinking down onto it. I look at her now, sitting astride me, my dick deep inside her, both of us fully dressed and I know she's the one for me. I know, I might have said those words before, but they weren't true before.

I trail my thumb along her jaw and then her bottom lip. She opens her mouth and sucks on it lightly, biting down as she rises up until just the head is in and then slams back down.

"Jesus, fuck," she says. "I get the awards ceremony, I really do. No one touches this dick but me now, is that clear?"

I nod and swivel my hips. My hand goes to the back of her neck and I pull her down for a kiss. "No one but you," I say hesitating, "and me?"

"Self-congratulations are encouraged, especially if you send me video, or better yet, do it live on a video call." Her eyes flutter as my hips try to move. "No more talking."

"Agree, no talking, more moving." My hands go to her hips again and I gently encourage her to move up and down, and she does. Simone rides me until she falls apart around me.

She's panting when I sit up a little, lift her off me and turn her so she's facing away from me. Lifting up her dress, I start to massage her ass cheeks, as I enter her again, inch by inch. Simone holds onto my legs for balance as I start to move her back and forth, watching my hard dick pump inside her. She takes over as I continue to knead her ass willing myself to last a little longer. My thumb wanders to where we connect, gathering some lubrication.

"Yes, Shel, yes," she says, looking back at me as my thumb enters her tight ass. Leaning forward, her hands on my shins now, she starts to fuck me harder.

The sight of her, head back in ecstasy, lit only by the intermittent flashes outside is enough to send me over the edge as I come harder than I thought possible. She continues to move her hips over me and as I feel her pulsing around my dick and my thumb. I press a little farther in as she continues to moan and convulse around me.

She collapses on my legs, her head between my feet, keeping our connection. I lower her skirt back over us, caressing and soothing her as she comes back to earth.

We lay like that for a few minutes, and even though it's weird, I like it.

Finally, she pushes herself back up, still fully seated on my semi-hard dick. She looks back at me with a huge smile. "How do you just know what I like, usually I have to beg a guy to do butt stuff, but you just know?"

I smile back at her and lift her off me so I can place her back in her original position of lying on top of me. Her hands go to my hair and I hug her close to me.

"I pay attention to the sounds you make, your face when I do certain things. When I brushed my finger over your ass and you made a happy sound, I felt it was fair game. I know you'd let me know immediately if it wasn't." I have very few sexual hang ups and anal sure isn't one of them. Most women aren't interested though, and I'd never try to coerce someone into something they weren't comfortable with, that's the opposite of fun for me.

"I love it," she whispers, "but I'm not sure about your monster going there, I'm not sure I'd be able to walk again."

I huff out a laugh. "Well, I've tried it once or twice, and it's tricky, but I was told it was worth it. We never have to do anything you wouldn't be 100% on board with, Simone."

"I know, you are the ultimate dirty gentleman." She rolls off of me and hops up. "I need to clean up, let's go to our room," she says and I get a tingle when she calls it, 'our room.'

Once we tidy up our messy selves, we curl up in my bed. Usually, we snuggle a little and then separate for sleep, tonight I'm having a hard time letting her go, so we fall asleep with her at my side, my arm tucking her into me.

CHAPTER 25

AU REVOIR

THE NEXT DAY is full of last-minute checks of Emilio's lip and the two tigers with seizures, getting Dr. Stevens ready to take over, and paperwork. I finally am able to start packing in the late afternoon and that's where Nancy finds me.

"Shel, I hate to see you go, but I'm so happy you were with us for all this time." Nancy sits next to my open duffle bag on the bed. The memory of having Simone sit on my face this morning in that exact spot reddens my cheeks. "I do hope you'll be able to visit again and maybe volunteer with us again soon."

"I'm honored to be here, Nancy, and I owe you and Nigel so much for this opportunity. It was truly a life-changing experience." I tuck my toiletries bag into the duffle then sit on the bed as well.

"In more ways than one, I imagine." I nod and look out the window. Kamal and Tasha are splashing around in the pond trying to bite a huge orange ball. It's too big and they can't get any purchase with their teeth. "Be patient with her, Shel, she's been burned badly and it's made her harder to reach, unfortunately. I can tell she fancies you more than she'll admit."

"I hope so because I really fancy her. I asked her to meet me in Paris, but I am worried it was too soon." I sigh and watch as Kamal jumps on the ball and ends up sinking.

I feel Nancy's hand on my shoulder and it's a comfort. Sometimes, I realize how much I missed growing up with parents like mine. They treat me like a friend now that I'm an adult. Their job is done, I safely grew up and moved away. If I asked my dad for advice, he'd laugh and say I knew my life better than he did, so why should he comment on it. My mom would recommend some essential oils and meditation.

"You are an extraordinary person who deserves the best in his life. I think Simone is the best woman for you, but only you and she know if that's true. You are both good people and if you make each other happy, then that's an awfully good start." She squeezes my shoulder and walks to the door. "Good things are coming your way, Dr. Locke, keep your eyes and heart open."

Dinner is a boisterous affair, with Nigel, Nancy, Dr.

Stevens and his wife, Marisa, Simone, chef, Bobby, and some of the other workers that I've spent a bit of time with. Chef prepares a huge traditional South African buffet (vegan of course). We drink way too much wine and when Chef rolls out a chocolate sheet cake with a tiger on it everyone cheers.

"Oh, this reminds me of when you got in the way of poor Kamal," Nigel says, barely containing his laughter.

"Bloody hell, Nige, don't ruin chocolate for me," Nancy scolds. "It's a beauty of a cake, chef, you've outdone yourself."

Chef asks and then Nigel regales him with the story of my brush with explosive tiger diarrhea. He and the other people who hadn't been there for it chuckle but look at me with a sort of respect. Nancy and Simone on the other hand, can't control themselves and are bent over in hysterics.

The rest of the night is full of more wine, and more roasting of yours truly. Simone tells them about our first meeting, and about all of my truck barfing. When she tells them about my hippo birth assist, Chef and Bobby look terrified.

"My brother was attacked by a hippo, lost his arm. Hippos are scary fuckers," Chef says and shivers.

Finally, I manage to say my goodbyes to everyone and head to my room. Nancy and Nigel are driving with me the four hours and we are leaving pretty early.

When I close my door, Simone comes through the

inner one wearing only her panties, holding two glasses and a bottle of champagne. I'm momentarily speechless because she is a vision, her creamy freckled skin glowing in the moonlight, her eyes clear and beautiful, and a huge smile on her face.

"This is what I want to walk in on all the time. You, half-naked with a bottle of champagne, I feel like I'm dreaming," I say while she uses the hand holding the champagne to push me to sit on the bed. She follows, sitting sideways on my lap, handing me the glasses to hold while she opens the bottle and fills them to the top.

A little spills on her and I take the opportunity to lick the bubbles from her perfect breasts. Maybe I'm overly thorough but who cares.

"Okay, Dr. Mini-perv, save some for later," she says and I move my lips to hers briefly before taking a large gulp of my drink.

We finish our glasses and she takes mine and puts them on the nightstand. "I want to celebrate with you, not have a sad goodbye, so I thought what's better than tits and champers?"

"I honestly can't think of anything better," I say laughing burying my face in her neck. "Hold on, I have a little speech prepared, and then we can move on to the debauchery."

"I'm certain I don't need the speech and would be happy to move on," I say moving my hand to graze over the front of her panties while dipping my head to suck on a nipple. My hand travels to the other breast as she presses my head away.

"Shel, please?" she asks sincerely so I stop and look at her. "I want you to know that this has been the best trip, and the reason it's been so great is you. I've been in a funk for a while and I'm happy I found the person to drag me out of it. You've changed me, and for that I'm thankful." She hops off my lap and then bends so her head is near my crotch. "I'd also like to thank you for your dedication, perseverance, and overall girth."

I laugh and pull her back to my lap. "I was not expecting that," I say.

"You're probably the first guy who's had two women give speeches to his dick. Lucky you," she says.

I lean my forehead to hers and hold eye contact. "You are the only one I want to talk to my dick, the only one I want in my life." I want to tell her I love her, but I'm afraid she'll get angry and blame it on our impending separation. I do though, I love her completely. "Please come to Paris," I add. "I left you the address of a cafe near my vacation rental. I'll be there every day at 4 pm, hoping to see you."

"Why not just give me the rental address?" she asks.

"What's romantic about that?"

"I'm a practical romantic, Shel, what if I'm late and can't meet you until the next day?"

"You do have my phone number so it's not totally up to chance," I say, "or you could go with it for me, the hopeless romantic."

She tilts her head and kisses me. I'll miss everything about her but her kisses the most. She tastes delicious, moves with my mouth like we are made for each other, and is really good at the little lip nibbles I like. After she kisses me thoroughly, I remember all the other things I'll miss.

I shed a few tears as pull away from the compound. When you have an experience like I have, it's hard to leave when you become attached to the animals you care for and successfully delivered to freedom.

"Aw, Shel," Simone says, hugging me to her.

"I love a proper sensitive man," Nancy says. "Nige is a crier too."

Nigel nods. "The first time we rescued a lion from a circus I broke down. I'll always be sensitive about that."

"Same here," I say watching my home for the past two weeks disappear as we go over the hill.

The rest of the drive is uneventful, I don't get car sick which is a relief to everyone and we stop and have a delicious lunch just outside of Johannesburg. My flight is still a few hours away so Nigel and Nancy drop us at the airport so I can check my luggage and have some time with Simone while they do some errands.

I check my duffle and we head to an outside café area near my terminal.

"Call me when you land in Dubai," Simone says, holding my hand. She hasn't let go of it since this morning. Again, I want to tell her how I really feel but I stop myself, too afraid of rejection.

"I will. Suzy has been there for a day already so I'm meeting her at the hotel." It's probably stupid to bring her up, but if it lights a fire under Simone to claim me, I'll try anything.

"She'll be somewhat over her jet lag too. I've never been there but it's a pretty fun party city, so I've heard." Her attention is on my hand she holds in hers so I lift it to my lips and her eyes follow.

"I wish you could come with me now, but just know that I'll be waiting for you in Paris," I drop her hand and kiss the side of her mouth, her cheek, and then full on the mouth. It's probably too much PDA but I don't care. We stay that way until my phone alarm goes off.

"You made this adventure great, it wouldn't have been as good without you," I say and wipe the tears falling on her cheeks.

She throws her arms around me and holds me tightly. I return the hug and stand up still holding her. We walk that way until we get to security and I place her back on her feet.

"See you in a week?" I ask, still paranoid because she hasn't given me a straight answer.

"See you in a week," she says and I feel a little better.

Walking away from her is hard and feels almost final. When I turn back, she's gone.

CHAPTER 26

DUDE BYE

EVERYTHING ABOUT DUBAI is over the top, that includes Suzy. She is waiting for me in the lobby of the giant resort holding a fruity drink. Her bright pink dress and giant white hat would make her stand out anyway, but her waving her free arm shouting my name draws all the attention to her. I'm laughing as I reach her and duck in for a hug, Suzy is at least a foot shorter than me and 100 times more frightening.

"Shelllllllly!" she calls. "It's so good to see your hot ass." She turns me around and smacks my ass.

"Suze, easy, let's not get arrested our first day here." I tap the brim of her hat and she backs off.

"Follow me, I already checked you in and have your key." Normally, we'd stay in the same room but Dubai is a different culture with different rules. The resort we are staying in caters to Brits and Americans so it's a little more relaxed, they also have a restaurant, bar, and nightclub all on premises. We don't need to leave if we don't want to, but we will explore the city tomorrow, according to the itinerary Suzy sent me.

The elevator is glass and faces out towards the city so the view is spectacular. I can also see some of the grounds, pools, and the Arabian Gulf beaches. It's so foreign to what my last month has been like it's over-whelming.

We disembark from the elevator and Suzy leads me to my room, scans the fob and opens the door with a flourish.

"Tada!" she exclaims waving her arms around. As I walk into the room, I see the giant aquarium across from the king bed. It's the entire wall and filled with tropical fish, and is that a turtle?

She jumps on the bed and crosses her legs, sipping from her drink as I walk to the window admiring the view of the city and the beaches. The hotel is located out on an island and faces the land.

"Dude, what is up?" Suzy asks as she now stands next to me.

"What? Nothing, I'm just tired and this is all so surreal. I was just in Africa and now I'm in weird Disneyland." I rest my head against the cool glass. The weather isn't usually too hot in February but today the temp is up there.

Suzy rests her head on my arm and I tuck her into

my side, she's so short that I can fit her under my armpit. I tried that exactly one time and am still recovering from the trauma to my nipple she almost twisted clean off.

"I'm glad you're here and I want to hear every last detail but you seem a little sad. Did your lady friend dump you before you got on the plane?"

I shrug my shoulders. "She might have, but I don't know. I asked her to meet me in Paris next week and she kind of said yes. I had the most amazing time and I think I finally found the woman for me. Unfortunately, she has commitment and trust issues."

"Ah, that old chestnut," Suzy says waving her hand. "If I had a dollar for every guy who dumped me with trust and relationship phobias, I'd be richer than I already am."

"I thought we worked through it, but as it got closer to me leaving, she pulled away a little." I was able to pull her back, especially with our physical connection but there was always some little nagging feeling that she was creating distance to protect herself.

"Classic girl about to be abandoned behavior. Whenever someone we really like has to go away we protect ourselves with aloofness to hide our panic." Suzy drains her drink and pushes my shoulder. "Go shower Africa off of you and meet me in the lobby in 20 minutes. We have drinks to drink and dinner to eat, and then dancing if you're up for it."

"I see you are doing fine with your jet lag?" I ask, knowing Suzy has the ability to rally in any situation.

"Naturally, dahling," she says. "Now go." She shoos me away and skips out of the room.

Our hotel has three bars, five restaurants and 20 pools. Because of liquor laws in the United Arab Emirates (UAE), alcohol can only be served and consumed in bars. This means any resort that caters to Americans and Europeans has to have bars so we can drink or as Suzy says, have our boozy vacay that is our god given right.

We sit in a bar that is open air to one of the pools and there is decent people watching. Suzy orders two of whatever she was drinking before and I don't mind. It's nice to sit and relax, no responsibilities for a while.

"So, tell me all about the perfect Simone." Suzy slurps her drink on purpose and rolls her eyes.

"She is perfect, for me. You would like her too, she's smart, loves Monty Python, and took absolutely zero of my shit."

"You don't really have much shit to take, but she does sound like someone I'd approve of." She tilts her drink to me. "Is she one of those save the animals, vegan nightmares?"

"No, she and I snuck out a few times and ate meat."

"Did she eat your meat?" Suzy asks and I see where I made my mistake.

I sigh and take a long sip of the delicious cocktail. "I should know better," I say to myself more than to her. "We had relations, but that's all the details you'll get about that."

Her mouth drops in mock shock. "As if I'd ever ask for such personal details."

"You literally texted me yesterday asking if her carpet matched the drapes," I deadpan.

"Yes, and I am still waiting on an answer." She taps her finger on her straw.

"Suze, she really is the one this time. I'm in love with her," I say making sure to look directly at her.

"Did you tell her that?"

"No," I say and curl into myself. "I was worried if I did it would scare her away for good."

"Or, she would know exactly how you feel and act accordingly."

I put my head in my hands. "I'm really trying not to fuck this up, in my usual fashion."

"I'm proud of your restraint, and I get your hesitation to let it all hang out there, but from what you've told me she really does like you for you," she says and I nod, knowing she's right.

"Ok, this is me promising you we are going to have a fun couple of days and I'm not going to fret about something that hasn't happened yet."

"Yes, let's tear this town up!" Suzy shouts and gets a scolding look from one of the employees. "Oops, I forgot I can't let my Jersey fly free here."

"How is everyone?" I ask and she starts telling me all about Dan and Cara's new baby and some of the improvements she's made on her beach house. All about her mother's broken arm from falling when their poodle got away.

"Maybe it's time for a miniature poodle?" I suggest.

"God forbid my mother change anything about her life. She hired a dog walker for Walter but walks with them. It's so weird." We both clink our glasses in solidarity of weird parents. "How are the Lockes?"

"Well, I got ahold of my dad about a week ago and he said they are sold out of all of their goat cheese and can't make it fast enough, also their angora rabbits are ready for shearing which to be honest, I'd love to see a video of my dad shearing a fluffy rabbit." My parents are constantly falling into dumb luck farming boons. If they were planning any of this they'd probably fail miserably, but somehow, they just decide to do something and it becomes the latest craze and then aren't prepared for it to take off. They make really good goat cheese and can never keep it stocked—a friend dumped a few rabbits on them last year and now they are the leading source of angora wool in New Jersey.

"They are always on the brink of success, just think

how much money they could make if they were half organized." She stares into space.

"I told him I was in South Africa and he seemed surprised," I say although it's not rare for my parents to forget to tell each other important news, or for them to just forget things in general.

We both laugh and order another round of drinks.

"So, what's the Paris plan?" Suzy asks after downing half of her new drink.

"I gave her a place to meet me where I'll be every day between 4 pm and 5 pm, although knowing me I'll stay until they close just in case."

She rubs her hand over her face. "Oh my god, Shel, just give her your address for fuck's sake. Why do you make everything so difficult?"

"I thought it would be romantic. I'll be waiting with a single rose and a bottle of wine and she'll walk up and we will be in Paris, Suzy. It's next level romance and will be a daily nightmare if she never shows." I hang my head because she's right, I'm being difficult.

"True romance isn't that extra, my dude. If she feels the same as you, it will be just as sweet if she shows up on your doorstep," she says making a good point. "Did you ever notice that Dubai sounds like dude, bye?"

"Aw fuck, that's the quote of the trip, isn't it?" I ask, knowing her answer. Whenever we go on a trip together Suzy comes up with some random yet related saying that becomes the quote of the trip because we start repeating it so constantly that almost all regular communication ceases.

"I'm still workshopping it," Suzy says, picking up her straw and putting it in her mouth to chew on. "I'm going to go see if our table is ready."

"Great, I'm starving."

"Hey," she calls and I turn to her. "Dude, bye." I laugh and shake my head.

The rest of our short trip is a fun distraction. We take a trip to the market, go snorkeling, swim in all twenty of the pools, and even dance at the club. I'm not much of a dancer, but Suzy loves it and uses me like a stripper pole. It'd be embarrassing to someone who had a shame gene, but not me.

She drops me at the airport and I'm a little sunburned, a lot relaxed, and very hungover.

"Listen Shel, Simone will show up, and if she doesn't, it's not a reflection of you. You deserve to be loved, and so does that beast in your pants." I put my hand over her mouth and she bats it away. "I know, I joke about it, but it's serious. I kick myself daily for not being able to force myself to love you. Some lucky girl will get to walk funny instead of me and it gives me nightmares."

"Thanks?" I tease and pull her in for a hug. "I love you Suze, and I'll see you this summer."

"Yes, I'm so excited for shore time with all of my friends!" Every summer we gather at her beach house for a week and it's always a good time. I never miss it. "Okay, I'm off, thanks for letting me crash your business trip."

"Always, big guy," she says and salutes me.

I turn to walk to security. "Oh, hey Suzy?" I call her and she turns back to me.

We both at the same time call out. "Dude, bye!"

CHAPTER 27

M'A POSÉ UN LAPIN

PARIS IS COLD AND RAINY. The weather matches my mood completely, as every day I've sat at this café alone, waiting like a fool for someone who is obviously not coming.

I walk the streets of Paris all day, only stopping for a quick lunch, and by four, I'm here at the same table, sipping a coffee or a large glass of wine. My waitress, Sylvie, tolerates my awful French until she puts me out of my misery and lets me know she speaks English.

On my last day, I stupidly show up and order wine and two croissants, a plain and an almond. I end up eating both and at some point, Sylvie takes pity and leaves the bottle of wine with me.

"Zees is your last day?" she asks, sitting across from me, something she's done a few times. Sylvie is exactly the type of girl I would normally move on with, but being with anyone but Simone feels wrong to me.

I nod and take a large gulp of wine. "Yes, and not a word from her."

"She is, how you say? Stupeed, beetch?"

I laugh but shake my head. "No, she's just afraid of me."

"You are monster?" she asks and her eyebrows raise. If Suzy was here, she'd do a spit take over the monster comment.

"No, I'm a good guy, she has been burned in the past and has a hard time trusting men."

Sylvie nods emphatically. "Ugh, I know zees, zees is me," she says, pointing to herself.

"I know it's hard but I love her and she knows deep down she can trust me." I finish my wine and pass Sylvie some Euros to pay my tab.

"I am finished with work. Do you want to come with me, Shel?" Sylvie half smiles and I know what this invitation means.

"You are nice to offer, Sylvie, but I'm going to pack and go to bed early."

She nods and places her hand on my forearm. "You pass zee test, Shel, I hope you find her at home."

We laugh and I walk her out where she will catch her bus. "Merci, Sylvie, Au revoir."

"Au revoir, Shel, and I hope we do meet again." She smiles showing teeth this time and waves me off.

My small apartment is nice but it feels very lonely. I can't for the life of me figure out why Simone would ghost me like this. At least if she wasn't coming, she could have let me know.

I send her a text. Something I haven't done all week.

Me: *I don't know what to say, except I miss you.*

I lay in the small bed staring at a water stain in the corner of the ceiling thinking about her. How she finally let her insecurities go the last week we were together. The looks she would give me from across a room, and her dedication to her work. I try not to think about her perfect face, her smile, the way she teases me, the nick-names she calls me.

My phone pings and I pick it up.

Simone: *I'm sorry. I got held up. Let's just call it a miss.*
Me: *What does that mean?*
Simone: *I think you know. We just want different things. I care about you but I don't think it will work.*
Me: *I'm sorry you feel that way, can we talk when I get back to CA?*
Simone: *I don't think that's a good idea.*

I'll be honest, I didn't see this coming. Sure, I

thought she'd want to take things slowly when we got back home, but not a complete freeze out. My heart is breaking and I don't know what I can do to change her mind. I type out and delete several texts until I finally just send her a broken heart emoji like some teenager.

The next morning, I wake up in a panic. I was having a bad dream. My mind was in the body of a tiger and I couldn't escape the cage I was in. After I calm my racing heart, I check my phone and there's nothing. I go through the motions of collecting my things, calling a car, traveling to the airport and boarding the plane and I feel numb.

How did things turn so bleak? Our separation at the airport was hopeful and I truly thought she'd meet me at the café.

I settle into my seat, I splurged for business class and I'm happy I did because it offers me some privacy so I can wallow without a chatty seatmate. The flight is long but direct so I settle in, watch a few movies, eat some barely edible food, and nap.

At the airport, I see a woman ahead of me in customs who looks like Simone. It's like my brain is trying to will her into existence. I look at my phone to distract me from hallucinating, checking on my social media pages that have blown up quite a bit since I've posted so much about my rescue trip. It doesn't make me feel any better.

Finally, it's my turn and while the official checks my passport, I glance up and see the redhead looking at me. She's quite a distance away, but she really resembles Simone. I shake my head and answer the lady checking me through. When I look back, the woman is gone. Is this my life now? Everywhere I look I'm going to see her?

My house is just the way I left it, cold and empty. Sure, I have furniture and art on the walls, but there's no one here to share it with me. In all the years of rejection, I've never taken it this hard and I need a friend.

Me: *Just got back, are you free for a quick beer?*
Frank: *Welcome back, cat boy, meet me at Finnegan's?*
Me: *See you in 20.*

Yep, my only hope to feel a little better is fucking Frank. At least that's what most of us call him. His grumpiness is legendary and his loyalty to friends is unshakable. I know he'll tell it to me straight, and give me the tough love I need to get over Simone. I can't tell Suzy, she will fly to San Francisco and tear Simone's heart out with her bare hands.

Finnegan's Wake is a classic neighborhood pub and Frank and I meet here a lot. I order a beer and grab a table between the pinball machines and pool tables. Normally, I'd be happy to pass the time playing a bar game, but nothing appeals. Even this beer feels flavorless and flat.

"Holy shit, man, you look like ass," Frank says as he sinks into the chair across from me, beer in hand. After he places it on the table, we do a little handshake and fist bump thing that Frank makes fun of me for forcing him to do, but is also secretly happy I don't want a hug like our friend, Joe insists on.

"Thanks, I feel like one too. This trip had some high highs but it ended very low." I explain all that went down between Simone and me and he lets me talk about it without interrupting. That's one of the things I appreciate about him as well. Suzy would have stopped me a few times to ask a question or make a comment, Frank just lets me get it all out there.

When I'm done, I take a big swig of my beer and wait for Frank's wisdom. He takes a big breath and socks me in the arm.

"That's a fucked up story," he says, rubbing his mouth with his hand like he doesn't want to tell me what he's thinking. He will though, and I appreciate the show of feeling bad about it. "Sheldon, I've known you for a few years now, and have witnessed your various poor choices in that time. You jump in too quickly, give away too much of yourself, and pick women that are all wrong for you. This time it seems like you did all the right things, waited for her to come to you, used your romance card, and gave her multiple orgasms. I can honestly say that this time I don't think it's you, it's her."

"So what can I do about it? I'm in love with her and she shut me out." I signal to the bartender and he brings us two more beers I may need a shot too if this gets more real.

"There's not much you can do other than wait for her to either come around or give you the final cutoff."

"How do I know that she hasn't already cut me off?" I ask.

"Her explanation is lame at best, she knows you deserve more, so I predict either a long email or a phone message detailing why she's dumping your ass coming soon." I definitely don't feel good about that.

"So, she'll give her reasons and I won't be able to give my rebuttal? That seems unfair."

"It is, so you'll have to manufacture a reason to see her. Does the rescue have offices in the city or Oakland?"

"Oakland, but it's rare that she is in residence there."

"Then you need reconnaissance. Get Nancy or Nigel on the line and get the information from them. Sounds like they are rooting for you." He has a point. I could get info from them and then go to the office when I know she'll be there.

"I like the way you think, Frank."

"Well, that makes one of you," he jokes and the only way I know this is the tiniest lift in the corner of his mouth. "You called me and not one of your other nerd friends because you didn't want me to hold your hand."

"Yep, tequila shot?" I ask and he nods.

The next morning, I wake to that email.

Dear Shel-

I know, email, how brave of me. I want you to know that I will always treasure our adventure together, especially South Africa. Maybe that's where we are meant to live on, in those memories. You woke me up from my fears and set me free. Unfortunately, I don't think we are right for each other.

I thought I could do it, could trust you and move forward. There are too many obstacles, too many doubts.

Hopefully, Paris was all that you hoped and you had fun in Dubai with your friend. I am sorry things didn't work out for us. When you see me again, let's be friends. I know it's not exactly what you pictured but it's all I can give you.

Sincerely,
Simone

Ugh.

How does one react to an email like that? There's no opening or place to work from. We aren't right for each other.

I pick up my phone and call Nancy. Time to bring in the big guns so I can whip a Hail Mary out of my ass.

CHAPTER 28

HIGH AND DRY

THE FREEDOM ROAR offices are located near the water and have a gorgeous view of San Francisco from their conference room windows. The sun is currently high in the sky here in Oakland but I can see the blanket of fog I left behind covering my adopted city.

"Sheldon," I hear Nancy call me before I turn to watch her float into the room. She's wearing one of her signature kaftans, her blonde hair cut into a sharp bob, much different from the high bun she wore for our trip. "You look wonderful, so good to see you. I'm sorry Nigel couldn't join us but he's still in South Africa settling Dr. Stevens in."

I welcome her warm embrace and smile as she beams up at me. "You are a vision, Nancy, I wouldn't even notice if Nigel were here."

She waves a hand at me. "You and your unicorn

business have no power here! How's it been settling backing real life again? Surely seems droll compared to your recent adventures. It's dangerous making a difference in the world, you get greedy for it."

"It's been good to see my friends and my regular clients, but you are right, I've been bitten by the adventure bug and I am ready to plan the next one." The first week I was home I felt invigorated by my travels, a new lease on life, despite my misery over Simone. To be back with animals, caring for them, gave me purpose and it felt good to be needed.

"A convert!" she exclaims and gestures for me to sit across from her. "Tell me why you came to see me, not that I'm complaining. A visit from you is always welcome."

"I was hoping to get more insight on Ms. Lyon." Nancy shakes her head. "I'm not looking for a mediator, or private information. My only interest is to talk to her, will she be in to work soon?"

"Oh dear, I don't want to interfere with you and Simone, but I know after Paris she was so disappointed, she flew back here, worked for a week, and then headed to London to see her father and meet with a group there that's working on the UK government legislation."

"What do you mean after Paris? She never showed up," I say completely confused. "I'm the one disappointed."

"Oh my, I thought you two had talked this out already," Nancy says not giving me anything more.

"You're right, I'm sorry to put you in the middle," I say. "Can I take you to lunch if I promise not to bring it up?"

"Of course dear, there's a new vegan spot I've been wanting to try. They have corn dogs and sausage rolls. Let's go," she says.

After my failed excursion to Oakland, I drive to Ocean Beach to clear my head. It's foggy and cold but it suits my mood. I check the time in London and decide it's not too late to call her. She answers on the third ring and it's hard to hear her with all the background noise.

"Shel?" she shouts into the phone. "Hold on."

I do and it gets a little quieter.

"Hey, Shel, I'm in a loud pub in London with my dad, is this important?" She sounds like she's sorry she answered the phone and maybe she made a mistake and didn't look at who was calling, I don't care, I'm going to take advantage.

"It is important to me," I say, take a big breath and go for it. "Did you come to Paris?" Now seeing her doppelgänger in the airport is starting to make more sense.

I hear her sigh. "Shel, I don't want to do this on the phone."

"Well, I don't want to do it this way either, but I'm going out of my mind trying to understand where I went wrong. I'm in love with you Simone and you not meeting me hurts. Help me." I know, I just can't hold it in, I love her and she needs to know.

"You're in love with me?" she asks and her incredulity gives me pause. "We were apart for a week before you went back to your old ways. Maybe sooner if you were sleeping with Suzy in Dubai."

What? "What?" I ask getting angry that she thinks I would ever sleep with another woman. "I have only been with you and only want you. How could you say that?"

"I saw you when I showed at the café, you and the blonde were all over each other, I even watched you leave together." Shit, Sylvie.

"That was not what you think, she was the waitress there and felt sorry for me."

"I can't do this, I'm hanging up," she says and disconnects the call. I try a few more times to call her until she obviously turns her phone off.

I leave her a short message again stating I only want her.

She must block me after that because I don't hear from her, and my calls and texts don't go through.

It's like she never existed at all. I send her an email and it bounces back. My last effort is to send my email explaining how I waited for Simone every day and that the woman she saw me with was the waitress and nothing happened with her, to Nancy. I get a simple response from Nancy saying she'd forward it along but that was the end of her involvement.

San Francisco gets a lot of rain in March and this one is no different. The rain and endless gloomy days match my overall mood. There are two times I feel better, one is when I'm caring for the animals at the clinic and the other is when I'm working on my new miniature series.

Each miniature is a character or scene from *Monty Python and the Meaning of Life*. I set them up and take photos. My Instagram has really blown up since I've been posting them and I even got a comment from a member on one of the photos. I'm going to try to tackle *Life of Brian* next.

Time marches on and my life is different. Where I used to go out almost every night, I rarely go out at all. My sex life is non-existent except for my solo escapades, and I haven't been on a date since before the trip. Frank tells me I need to mourn the end of my relationship with Simone, but I feel like we left things so unfinished, it's hard to close that chapter.

Suzy encourages me to get back out there so in late June, I find myself waiting for a woman I've been chatting with on a dating app. We are meeting at one of my favorite restaurants, Cha Cha Cha on Haight St., a fun tapas restaurant with the best sangria in town.

Fran meets me in front of the restaurant and I already know I'm not ready. She's a beautiful woman and normally I'd be imagining our future together before we even enter the restaurant but all I can think about is that she's not Simone. The hostess seats us and we order sangria and I already know I'm going to drink more than I should.

"I love this place, it's nice to come for lunch when it's not so busy," Fran says and I nod in agreement. "Do you come here a lot?"

"More than I should, but I live a few blocks away so it's a little too convenient." She smiles at me and our waiter drops chips and salsa on our table, ready to take our order.

I don't remember most of the date, and I feel like a complete asshole.

"I feel like a total asshole, but I don't think I'm ready to date yet," I say as we order another round after eating way too much food. "You seem awesome and I feel awful for wasting your time."

"I got a weird vibe from you and I'm glad you told me," she says very gracious about it all. "It's so difficult to date in this city and you seem like a seminormal dude, whoever you're hung up on is a lucky lady."

"My friends would not consider me normal so I look forward to letting them know you think that," I say dodging the lucky lady comment. "I guess I've made one too many miniatures of their pets, or every kind of sushi to find me normal."

We chat a little more about my hobby and she asks about the trip and saving the big cats. I never get tired of talking about my adventures with Emilio, Gloria, Kamal, Tasha, and all the others. I tell her about my brush with projectile tiger diarrhea and we both laugh. It's nice to laugh with someone.

"Shel, can I keep you as a friend?" she asks.

"I'd like that, I can always use a new friend."

We exchange numbers and part ways, her in an Uber and me on foot back to my empty house. My phone dings as I grab a beer out of my fridge. I'm going to get day drunk and no one can stop me.

Suzy: *Shelly bell, how are you doing?*
Me: *Fucking great!*
Suzy: *No, you are not good at the sarcasm, I can't tell if you're serious.*
Me: *I had three drinks on my lunch date and now I'm home having number four.*
Suzy: *See, I still can't tell. Did the date go well?*
Me: *It was fine, she was too good for me.*

Suzy: *Obviously, most women are. I'm sorry?*
Me: *I'm not over Simone, I can't think about anyone or anything else.*
Suzy: *Oh Shelster, why can I do?*
Me: *Go to London and insist she listen to reason?*
Suzy: *I mean, you could do that?*
Me: *I have no idea where she is, it would be a disaster. I don't think I can handle more rejection on foreign soil.*
Suzy: *These are good points. I wish I could fix things for you. You are one of the best men I know and you deserve all the happiness.*
Me: *I wish you could too, I'll be okay, eventually.*

As the months go by, missing Simone gets easier, but I still feel the hole she left behind. Making my new miniature series of broken-hearted self portraits has gone somewhat viral on my Instagram and apparently there are several TikTok pages dedicated to me. If it wasn't so pathetic, I might actually be cool with it.

I start to add a redhead to my series, but the two never meet or touch. This series goes seriously viral and I'm set to be interviewed by the local news later this week. It's my favorite time of year in the city. San Francisco always has the best weather in October. The city almost sparkles into sunlight.

My interview goes well and business at the clinic picks up a little, allowing me to bury myself in work, instead of pining. Frank tells me it's embarrassing to still be holding a torch for Simone, and I remind him of his long unrequited torch for his friend Lia. There was mumbling and a middle finger pointed in my direction.

It's Friday and after my shower, I go through my mail. It's mostly bills but there's one envelope that stands out. It's orange with tiger stripes. When I open it I'm met with an opportunity. The invitation is for Halloween and it's the Freedom Roar party. I'd forgotten all about it but I am happy to be invited, knowing that Simone will most certainly be there.

So will I.

CHAPTER 29

HE DID THE MASH

THERE IS nothing I love more than a costume party. I wouldn't call myself shy, but I can be a bit of an introvert so a costume affords some armor and I've always loved to go out as someone else. Today I have some actual armor as I'm dressed as Sir Robin from *Holy Grail*. My hope is to make Simone laugh. I even have a coconut split in half tied around my waist to make horse hoof sounds.

The party is in a ballroom at the Fairmount Hotel, a very fancy place for an animal rescue to throw a party, but Nancy tells me one of the hotel owners is a huge donor and donates the room, food and labor for the evening. I'm sure people like MJ and Joe are also happy to contribute to events like this.

"Look at this guy," someone says behind me and speak of the devil, it's Joe. He is dressed as Marc

Antony and the lovely MJ is a gorgeous Cleopatra. "I almost said you were Lancelot but I see the coconuts and you must be Brave Sir Robin."

MJ rolls her eyes. "This man is a sucker for the *Holy Grail.* I love that you and Simone's costumes match. You must have missed her so much while she was in London."

My smile probably looks weird but I have a lot of conflicting emotions. I recognize that they don't know that we aren't together, and I hate to let them think that. That Simone is around here somewhere wearing a costume that matches mine warms my heart a little.

"Yes, I missed her very much," I say and that's no lie.

"MJ and I have been following your miniature collections and are huge fans. If you ever want to leave the vet game and move to Hollywood, there's a need for miniatures in movies all the time," he says, grabbing glasses of champagne off a passing tray and handing them to MJ and me. "There's been talk of you doing some modeling too, let me know if you need any agent contacts."

I shake my head, he's right I've had a lot of offers, but I have zero interest, and not a lot of time to pursue a side hustle.

"I guess I could really chuck it all and head down to LA for a modeling and miniature making career." I clink my glass to theirs and we all laugh.

"You really could, you are a hot commodity right now. If you wanted, you could make a ton of money."

"Joe, I'm sure he knows all of this, plus he looks overwhelmed so maybe we could roll back the commodity talk?" She gives me an apologetic look. "Any adventure trips coming up, Dr. Locke? I know Nigel has trips planned to Brazil and Argentina. They have some local jurisdiction bans, but we are trying to get national bans."

Nigel has sent me an email or two asking if I'd be willing to travel with them again, but no definite plans. "I'm always up to travel with the cats and set them free where they can live comfortable lives."

"I heard the lion cubs are doing well, and that Quique has calmed down some in his old age." It's nice to hear this news from Joe. I do get some updates from Dr. Stevens and Bobby, but they are brief and sporadic. "One of the female tigers had some surgery, but other than that they all seem to be living the good life."

"I'm so happy to hear it. They were all so easy to get attached to and I miss them."

A new couple dressed as Harry Potter and Ron approach MJ and Joe and I take my leave. I wander around admiring the beautifully set tables and checking out the silent auction area. I bid on a Galapagos trip I probably won't get, but has always been a dream excursion. I think most vets would love to travel there.

The music gets a little louder before it's turned down

completely and someone calls us to dinner. I have my place card and go to my assigned table. There are about eight other people at the table and everyone is dressed in amazing costumes. There are mermaids, pirates, Victorian ladies, a cowboy, and an Austin Powers so good that I think it might actually be Mike Myers.

I introduce myself to the mermaid to the left of me and the cowboy to my right. We chat about everything and nothing while eating a delicious mushroom appetizer, a beet salad and a main course of creamy pasta with butternut squash. It's all delicious and of course, vegan.

After dinner is cleared and before dessert is served, someone taps on a microphone and asks for our attention. This person is dressed in a fluffy white rabbit costume, has blood on its fur and fake fangs. This person is Simone. I get it now. She's dressed as the killer bunny.

"Just a harmless little rabbit," I mumble to myself.

"Good evening all you monsters," Simone says and everyone claps. "We at Freedom Roar are so thankful that you could attend our Halloween gala this year. It's our fifth annual party and the biggest one yet."

She goes on to thank a long list of donors, volunteers, and of course Nigel and Nancy.

"Last winter we completed our third large rescue of circus lions and tigers and brought 17 of them all the way from Guatemala to our South African reserve. In addition to those cats, we found a lioness and her cub and reunited them with her mate in Colorado." The entire room is mesmerized by her and I'm not surprised. Even in that ridiculous costume, she's like a beacon and all eyes are on her.

"The fight still persists and more donations are needed to keep the animals that we've rescued fed and safe, and for the rescues from countries that are enacting bans. We have trips planned to both Brazil and Argentina to tighten up their laws and get them passed. So many countries are on board, but we won't rest until all wild animals are free from abuse and neglect." She goes into detail about our Guatemala rescue and how the Brazil fight is similar.

A screen lowers arm the ceiling and the room darkens. "Please enjoy this documentary about our amazing rescue and transport of the Guatemala lions and tigers."

The footage begins to roll and as much as I want to hide from it, I stay and watch every second. All of the memories of that trip come flooding back as I watch footage of the earlier rescues before I arrived, to the rescues I participated in. What really gets me though, is the footage of us releasing the cats in South Africa. The pure joy of all of us lifting those heavy doors and letting the lions and tigers free is infectious.

While the documentary plays, I steal glances of Simone. She sits on the side of the stage, enjoying the film. It's almost as if she's purposefully not looking in my direction. I'm here, and she knows it. She may have already clocked me when I arrived. While Nigel speaks animatedly about the people caring for the cats at the refuge, I stare as hard as I can at Simone in her ridiculous bunny costume.

Then comes the tour of the lodge, highlighting the teaching aspect and showing the observation room in detail. I can't think of a room I have more fond feelings for, except maybe that cargo bay where we made love for the first time. Even from this distance, I can see Simone's cheeks flush. She runs a hand over her forehead, wiping sweat from her brow. It's nice to know she remembers.

God, she's stunning, even in the white fluffy outfit and sharp fangs. I really hope I get a chance to talk to her, even if it's short.

The movie ends and Simone returns to the podium.

"Thanks so much to Joe and MJ Hales for not only their large donations every year, but for making these films. They are so important in getting information out about the work we do, and show the real results we've accomplished. Please give a round of applause to our favorite benefactors." She points to MJ and Joe at a table near the front of the stage and they both shyly wave, until Nigel forces them up out of their seats to receive their recognition.

After a few minutes, the crowd calms back down, and Simone proceeds. She talks about the silent auction and encourages people to bid. I think she's done and can't wait to seek her out, but she flips the card her speech is most likely written on and gestures to someone backstage.

"Every year we give an award to someone who went above and beyond in our organization. This year's recipient is extraordinary. He was the comic relief, the glue that kept us together, and did some things that went far above and beyond what was required. This person was on the receiving end of a lot of crap, and I mean that literally." I laugh nervously because there's no way she can be talking about anyone but me. "He showed up on camp the first day, jumped in and was all in for the duration of our trip. The dedication, warmth, humor, and love this person brings made the trip even more amazing. Not only did he treat the animals in our care, but was called to a local zoo to help with a hippo birth."

The crowd oohs and ahs as she regales them with stories of the rescues, how I repaired Emilio's lip, administered medication while flying, and of my bloody incident with the Mexican authorities.

"All of these things make our Dr. Locke a special person. We were so lucky to be able to work with him. I was lucky to be loved by him," she says and now the audience is so quiet you could hear a mouse squeak. "That's right, we fell in love. Cat camp is an intense place and feelings get amplified quickly. What I thought was just an adventurous fling, turned into something much more."

I've been staring at her since she got on stage, so when she turns to look at me our eyes lock. "Sheldon Locke, you are something special and this year's recipient of the Cat Camp Spirit award." She holds out the glass tiger mounted on a small piece of wood.

There's no other option except to go up and accept the award. I'm sure my face is frozen in some shocked expression as I get up from the table and make my way up onto the small stage.

"Here he is, oh and look, our costumes match!" Simone says clapping as I make my way to her.

We lean in and hug, she smells like roses and lemons. All I want to do is pull her to me and never let go. Unfortunately, she steps back and gestures to the microphone. I guess I'm going to make a speech now— not sure if my voice is working but I'll try,

"Hi there, I'm Sheldon Locke and it's an absolute honor to not only be here tonight, but to have been a part of such a life-changing adventure." I look at Simone and she is smiling at me and it seems sincere. "I've been obsessed with animals my whole life, but I am usually around dogs and cats. To be with these majestic tigers and lions for a month was intense, and as Ms. Lyon told you they all left a mark on me, some of them literally."

Again, I turn to Simone and hold out my hand. To

my shock, she takes it and stands closer to me. "Meeting this woman and spending time with her was the absolute highlight. I've never met someone as smart, funny, and hardworking as Simone Lyon. She is my match, my soul mate, and I never want to part from her again." Tears are streaming down her face and it feels like we are the only ones in the room.

"Kiss her already, Locke," Nigel calls out and I laugh because we are definitely not the only ones in the room.

Turning back to the audience, I hold the tiger to my chest and say thank you. The crowd claps but Nigel starts a chant of "kiss her" so in order to restore the peace to the now rowdy crowd dressed as animals, pirates, superheroes, etc., I lean down and kiss Simone on the cheek. This gets a few boos but we leave the stage and Simone pulls me through a door and into a small room with a few couches and a large fireplace.

"Hi," she says still holding my hand she leads us to one of the couches and we sit side by side.

I stare at her, nose covered in black make-up for her bunny look, terrifying sharp teeth and I've never been happier to see anyone in my whole life.

"Hi," I say back, reaching to tug on her bunny ear. "This costume is frightening. Well done."

"Shel, I'm sorry. I messed up, and I'm sorry."

My hand travels to cup her cheek and she leans into my touch. "I accept any and all apologies."

She shakes her head. "You shouldn't, I was horrible to you and then I lost my sense of what was real, I didn't trust you and that was all my fault. You've always been honest with me, even when it made you not look so great. When I got to the café in Paris and saw you with that woman, I used it as an excuse to leave. In my heart, I knew you were only being friendly, that you were true to me."

"I was, I only see you, Simone, only you," I say, cradling her face with both hands.

"The pictures and videos of your miniatures made me realize how much I meant to you. I finally read your emails and then I felt so foolish." I wipe tears from her cheeks, trying to avoid smudging her drawn on whiskers. "The only way to mend us was for me to make a spectacle of myself. How did I do?"

"You did perfect," I say and dip down and touch my lips to hers. "I love you, Simone, so much." It feels good to say it to her. I never want to stop saying it to her. "I love you."

"I know you do, and even though I'm late to the love party, I love you too, Shel." I kiss her again, this time deepening it a little.

There's a knock at the door. "What now?" I ask.

She winks at me and gets up to answer the door.

CHAPTER 30

THE MONSTER SMASH

NIGEL, Nancy, MJ, and Joe are some of my favorite people. Right now, they are not. They all bust into the room and are all talking at once. It's overwhelming, but they are all in good spirits and seem genuinely happy for us.

Nigel sits next to me and pats me forcefully on the back. "Good show, you were a shoo-in for the award."

Nancy rolls her eyes. "You chose him, you wanker."

"Did you offer him the job yet?" MJ asks.

"No, because you all have zero chill and gave us like five minutes to talk," Simone teases.

"Didn't sound like anyone was talking when we knocked," Joe says wiggling his eyebrows.

"You are going to offer me a job?" I ask.

"We want you to be our permanent travel vet," Nancy says clapping her hands. "It would mean a lot less time at your clinic but more consistency in the care the cats get."

I nod because I have no idea what to say.

"It's a lot right now," Nigel says, his hand still on my back. "You think about it and spend some time with this one." He gestures to Simone and then gets to his feet. "Come on you lot, let's leave these two alone so they can get to shagging."

Simone turns a dark shade of pink as Nancy scolds Nigel and shepherds him out of the room. I can't stop smiling and haven't been able to since Simone told me she loved me. I feel like I'm in a dream right now. She is sitting across from me, her head in her hands looking a little stressed.

I settle down next to her and pull her into my lap, a move I know she loves. "Hey," I say pulling her hands away so I can see her beautiful face. "How are you?" I ask because I want to know in general but also specifically right now, how she is doing.

"I'm okay, but I think I'm crashing because I was so nervous before. Now that you're here, and you're mine, I feel happy and relieved." She brushes the hair out of my eyes. "The whole event has spun me into a mess though. I don't know what I was thinking."

"That you wanted to make sure I listened?"

"Yeah, I really did."

"Simone, I want you to listen too. I've never felt this way about anyone, and never once did I try to find it elsewhere. You are everything for me, the whole taco."

She laughs. "I think the saying is the whole enchilada," she says tapping her finger to her lips.

I shrug. "Tacos are better."

"I won't argue that point," she agrees and snuggles into my chest. I hold her there for a while, just happy to be close.

"Do you have to stay much longer?" I ask, hoping that I'll be able to steal her away.

"No, the speech and documentary were my big tasks for the evening. The silent auction is being run by Sarah who works at the office in Oakland."

"Good," I say and stand with her still in my arms. "This is going to be interesting."

The door wasn't closed all the way so I'm able to kick it open. We proceed back out into the crowd, where people are dancing, drinking, and making merry. Many of those people stop to watch the giant knight carry the white bunny across the ballroom, out to the street. We get a lot of supportive cheering.

It's quiet the entire cab ride to my house as we just sit and stare at one another. I'm sure we are making our driver sick with our cheesy heart eyes but I don't care. Our hands are entwined on the seat between us and we are happy to just breathe each other in.

After we enter my house, there is still silence as we make our way up the stairs to my room. I take off my "armor" and strip down to my boxer briefs. Simone, too busy watching me is still in her bunny suit.

I crook my finger at her and she walks to stand between my legs. The zipper is hidden at her neck but I find it and pull it down. My jaw drops as I realize she's wearing nothing but a matching white lace bra and panties. She steps out of the suit and removes the ears.

When her hand goes to her teeth, I stop her. "Leave the fangs." She laughs and all of the tension drains from the room. We both fall to the bed and laugh until she starts hiccupping.

"Shel, I missed you," she says straddling me and pushing me flat on the bed.

Her eyes sparkle with tears from our laughing fit and I can hardly believe this is real. She bends to kiss me and my hand goes to the back of her head to hold her to me. There's nothing better than kissing Simone. She has perfect lips and her tongue is the best thing ever.

We kiss long and lazy, my hands traveling to her hips, toying with the lacy strap of her thong. I give it a little tug and she gasps.

Her hips slowly drag back and forth creating friction that drives us both wild. Gently, I roll us on our side so I can remove her bra and both of our underwear so we are completely naked. I stroke up and down her side, her skin is so soft until my fingers create goosebumps.

"I don't need to go slow, Shel. We can do slow later," she whispers and I agree by throwing her on her back, rubbing my hard dick over her wetness, then entering her fully. "Oh, shit, maybe a little warning would have been good."

I grind myself into her pelvis and she rolls her hips to meet me. Slowly, I drag myself out so just the tip is inside her, then slowly sink back in. "Is that better?" I ask, barely able to speak I'm so turned on.

She shakes her head. "Nope, stop listening to me and just do your thing."

I lean in so my mouth whispers along the shell of her ear. "I'll always listen to you, especially when you tell me to do my thing." She is panting now and so I put her out of her misery and start to move faster, still kissing and nibbling her ear.

Going slow wasn't my plan but I find myself savoring every bit of her. I understand the compulsion to bang one out since we are both clearly needing to get off, but I also haven't seen her in months and I don't want to miss anything about this experience.

Her legs are wrapped around my waist as I pick up the pace a little and then slow it down. I can tell she's getting frustrated because she squeezes me with her legs. "So impatient, I thought you were going to let me do my thing?"

"Shel, you are far too good at fucking me, and I have no argument except I need you to go a little harder," she punctuates this with a slap to my ass.

"Harder?" I ask playfully, sitting up on my knees

and pushing her legs back wide, my hands on the back of her thighs. This is the yawn position and it's one I love because I can see everything that's going on, and I am able to play with her clit while fucking her. It allows me to not only go hard but deep as well.

I don't hear a word from her after that. She dissolves into a sexy mess, her whole body flush, her breaths coming quick, her orgasm rippling through her body. My thumb keeps pressure on her center, keeping her in the orgasmic state while I feel my own tell-tale tingles up my spine.

We lay in a heap, letting the cool air settle over our nakedness, Simone is tucked into my side, and I have one hand in her hair, the other stroking her hip. I can't stop touching her and she must have a similar compulsion as she runs her hand over my chest.

"How do you have so many muscles that I didn't even know existed?" she asks, fingers circling my obliques.

I smile, but I've been smiling since she said she loved me, on stage, in front of a big crowd of people. "My body developed through farm work, once I left the farm my exercise changed but the muscles didn't. I got more flexible from yoga, and I have more stamina from doing cardio, but I've been this way since I was 18."

"Farms are underrated hot dude factories."

I laugh. "Well, if you're the only unpaid farmhand

on your hippie parents' farm you are going to be a little muscular. I don't know about the hot part."

Simone pinches my nipple. "Don't make me hurt you, Dr. DNA. You know you're hot and it's not a good look when you deny it. Being hot is the least interesting thing about you."

"I've heard that somewhere. Please tell me all the things you find interesting about me."

She rolls on top of me, straddling me naked, now I really don't care what she finds interesting.

"You have a kind heart, you know how to work hard. Even when you are covered in shit, your goodness shines through. The things you say to me, you are honest, there's no pretense. There's so much more, but the orgasms, the multiple orgasms you give me make me feel like I'm the only woman in the world." She punctuates this last point by sliding up and down my hardening dick.

My hand glides up to cover her heart. "This is precious to me and I'll do whatever it takes to make sure you feel my love, whether it's through the multiple orgasms, or supporting you when you need me. I can't help showing my love for you, because you are every-thing to me."

She sighs leaning down to kiss me. We get lost in each other again and I make sure she feels my love multiple times.

One of my greatest wishes happens the next day as we wake up in my bed together.

"All I've wanted was to have you here, in my home, waking up with me," I tell her.

"Ugh, we have to wake up?" she mumbles as I pull her to me, her back to my front.

"You might want to be awake for what's about to happen," I tease as I move down her body then swing her leg over so she's spread out before me. She opens one eye but is smiling. When I run my tongue over her center, she shivers and closes the one eye.

"Mmm, awake sounds good."

We spend the morning in bed, shower together, and I make us some omelets.

"Tell me more about the job," I say and take a bite of her toast.

She smiles wide and claps. "Nancy and Nigel made this job specifically for you, when they presented it to me, I knew they had ulterior motives. By then, I'd seen your news interview and all of your Instagram posts. I knew you were obsessed with me and the only way to cure you was to put you out of your misery and jump you. The job was a bonus. It killed me to wait until the gala but Nancy convinced me it would be worth the big gesture."

"Was it?" I ask.

"Shel, you are worth it all. You deserved that flashy declaration for what I put you through. I'm sorry I hurt you. I needed to get over all my bullshit before I could give myself to you fully." She steals her toast back.

"It did hurt, but I understood and still do, because you are worth it too," I say and we sit there like fools smiling and staring into our futures.

EPILOGUE

SIMONE

A few years later…

There is literally no one as hot as my husband. It took me a while to adjust to his beauty, his big heart, those abs. He's a lot to take in but I do my best every day to make sure he feels how much I love him.

We are at the Freedom Roar lodge again having just delivered our third group of big cats to the reserve since that first trip. Things seem to be moving in the right direction in most countries but we have a lot of work to do still. I wish I could say Sheldon has gotten better at rescue missions but he is still a hot mess in a truck, and not comfortable with guns pointed at him.

Shel and I spend half of our year traveling and half in San Francisco plotting our next trip while he helps out his old clinic a few days a week. It's a fun but exhausting way of life but we are both dedicated to saving as many animals as possible.

I'm hoping he will be willing to put that on hold for at least a year.

I find Shel in our bed, taking a break from the heat. I climb in next to him and snuggle up. "Hey, Dr. Mini-perv, how's my best guy?"

"Always better when you are in my arms," he says, and yes, the swoony stuff he says still makes my heart flutter.

"Did you see Quique? I bet he missed you." He's still sensitive about the big ornery tiger.

"Yeah, this time he didn't try to electrocute himself on the fence so baby steps I guess?" He rubs his chin. "I'm worried about Fabia, her seizures haven't improved and they had to revive her last month. She's been inside under observation since then."

I hug him hard. The way he loves these animals kills me. "She's had the best life for the past three years and I'm sure she'll bounce back."

"You're right, I just hate that there's nothing I can really do to help her." He squeezes me harder.

I pull back and kiss his chin. "I have a surprise for you," I say and he rolls to his side so we face each other.

"Nothing will ever compare to the surprise of you in

my life, I still can't believe you married me," he says and I know, the things he says are just panty melting. It should be corny but his 100% sincerity sends it straight to my soul. I wipe my eyes and feel a little foolish at the way he affects me.

"Simone, why are you crying?" he asks kissing my tears away, then kisses me properly on the mouth. "I hate to see you sad."

I sit up and he does too. "I'm not sad, I'm unimaginably happy."

He pulls me into his embrace and holds me like I'm the most precious thing in his life. I know I am and I'm looking forward to sharing that title.

"Come on, I need to show you your surprise," I say standing and pulling him with me.

We walk up the stairs to the observation room, the room we both love so much, we got married here. It was a small ceremony since getting people to travel to South Africa is a big ask, but we had our families there and a few friends. Shel surprised me with a big wedding reception when we got back to San Francisco and both of those days are special to me.

The room is lit up with giant lanterns I bought in town and there's a small table set for two. I got Chef to make the same taco buffet he made for us a few years ago and it smells heavenly in here.

Shel squeezes my hand. "I love it." He turns to me and holds me close. "I love you, my lioness."

That's his joke nickname for me because of my last name. Listen, he can't be all perfect, it's already way too much.

We pile up our plates and eat more tacos than should be eaten by two humans but they are so good it's hard to stop. The room is dimly lit so we can watch Kamal and Tasha play. They are thriving here after three years and are everyone's favorite. Maybe it's because they are closest to the lodge, but it could be their sweet temperament or playfulness with each other. They are true soulmates and are enjoying their freedom to the fullest.

After dinner, we settle into our favorite couch to enjoy the view as it starts to storm. Storms in South Africa are full of drama and huge bolts of lightning. We don't get a lot of thunderstorms in the Bay Area so we really enjoy them when we are here.

This is what complete happiness feels like. I'm sitting in my favorite place next to the man of my dreams and I'm about to blow his mind. Not like that you dirty birds—well maybe after.

"I love being here with you, it's like this room belongs to us. We have so many great memories tied to this place," Shel says and my heart overflows with love for him. We are pretty gross, I know.

I sit up and sit to face him. "That's why I wanted to be here when I told you that you're going to be a dad."

The look on his face is like a kaleidoscope of

emotions. He goes from shock to happy to emotional to lust and back around to happy.

"Wow, there's a lot going on in there," I say leaning in to kiss his forehead. "You look happy though, and that's what I was hoping for."

He grips my hips and pulls me to his lap. "I didn't think it would be possible to be happier, it almost feels wrong to be this happy. We're having a baby?"

I nod and kiss his tears now and wipe my own away. "I found out right before we left for Argentina but wanted to wait to tell you until we got to our room."

His look changes to worry and I knew he was going to fret over me, this was another reason I wanted to tell him.

"Are you sure it was okay to do all the traveling and sleeping on a cot," he says getting all worked up. "Wait, you went on rescues, that's not safe."

I stop him with a kiss. "Shel, I'm fine, I checked with the doctor before I left and I tried to let you and everyone else do the heavy lifting, I was hoping you wouldn't notice and think I was being lazy. I always stayed in the truck for the rescues, I promise." I poke his chest and he deflates.

"All this time I could have been spoiling you and I missed it?"

"Sweet man, I'm only four months so you have five to six more to cater to my every whim."

"Good, I already have a few ideas," he says and I

kiss him again pressing down on his erection. I'm wearing my favorite kaftan with nothing on underneath, just for him. If you haven't experienced the comfort and accessibility that a kaftan provides, I suggest you go out and get one as soon as you are able.

"I have ideas too," I say gathering my dress to my waist so I'm bare on his dick which is covered only by his light sweatpants. He stills my hips and lifts me up to free himself from said sweats.

As I sink down on him, I count my lucky stars that not only did I find the most considerate and sexy guy but that he has been endowed with the most magical penis. I had an orgasm once just seeing him take it out of his pants.

We sit connected and he cradles my face in his giant hands, a move I never get tired of. He kisses my chin and works his way down my throat to my collar bone. His hands lightly caress my sensitive breasts.

"These did seem a bit different but I didn't want to mention it." He dips his mouth to my nipple and kisses me there. I wiggle in his lap, needing to move but his hands are still holding my hips, keeping him fully seated inside me. I love feeling so full of him but I feel a bit frantic and need him fuck me.

"Another thing that may be a bit different is I'm beyond horny and you need to fuck me now."

"No slow?" he asks smiling at me.

"Nope," I clip out and start rolling back and forth on him.

"I've got you," he says in an almost purr, and holy shit, am I coming already?

He holds me close as I convulse around him.

"That's one," he teases. Sometimes he counts how many times he can make me orgasm and who am I to get in the way of his goals?

He lifts me off him and arranges me on my stomach so my head rests on one pillow and then props my hips up on two more. My ass is up and his for the taking, and take he does. Instead of putting his dick in me, he decides to use his tongue and all coherent thought leaves me.

Shel sucks on my clit while dipping a few fingers inside me. His pinky finger brushes my ass and he knows this drives me crazy. I'm about to come on his face as he removes the fingers from my pussy and breeches the other hole. It doesn't stop my orgasm but accelerates it and makes it more intense.

He pulls back and swats my ass. "Two," he says proudly.

My hips are lifted off the pillows as Shel spears me with that giant dick again. He's always been a lot to take but from behind it feels even fuller.

"You need me to fuck you, Simone?" he asks and I can barely nod. He laughs and holds my hands at my lower back. I love when he does that and I feel another orgasm coming for me as he pounds me into the couch.

It barrels through me and I can tell he's close too because he's making his hot sounds he makes right before he comes. He smacks my ass again and I make some sort of noise that must spur him on because he thrusts into me a few times then pulls out and comes all over my ass.

"Jesus, you are the hottest pregnant woman, I wish I could knock you up again." I laugh at this as he rubs his come over my ass, dipping his finger in and out, as I push into his caresses.

"Let's get this one out into the world before we talk about another."

He gets up and finds some napkins to tidy me up, then pulls my kaftan back over my head so I'm not cold. He takes care of me when I need it and I know he'll be the best dad.

"You're going to be the best dad," I say out loud.

"Only because I already love you more than is appropriate so now, I can spread some of it out to our child." How did I get so lucky?

"We are lucky to be loved by you," I say and kiss him, trying to send every overwhelming feeling I have to him.

He smiles because he doesn't know what to say for that and I love him even more.

ACKNOWLEDGEMENTS

In January 2020, a dear friend of mine embarked on a trip of a lifetime. We followed his adventures closely as he posted them on his social media. My family and I were obsessed. He was saving these lions and tigers and bringing them to a place of freedom.

This book is wholly dedicated to my friend Howard Rosner and his amazing experience with Animal Defenders International (ADI). In fact, I could give him partial writing credit for all the great stories he sent me.

So many thanks to ADI for all of their amazing work. Please check out their website and follow along what those real lions and tigers are doing in South Africa now.

https://www.ad-international.org

I will be donating 20% of all proceeds from this

book towards adopting one of the animals. I'll keep you posted!

This year was a weird one, but I am still able to feel inspired and hopeful.

Thank you to Andrew, Maggie, and Buster for being my home team forever.

Thanks to other authors who wrote such beautiful and amazing books for me to distract myself.

Thanks to Karen Hulseman for taking on this beauty of a cover and making it shine.

Thanks to Keith Manecke for that face, that body, and the kindness that shines through.

Thanks to Christopher Correia for the gorgeous photo.

Thanks to Meaghan Royce for fixing my comma problems, and putting up with my sporadic requests.

Thanks to all my readers, I appreciate you so much and hope you are okay. Make sure to take care of yourself.

Jen Luerssen grew up in New Jersey and then lived for 20 years in the San Francisco Bay area. She has held various jobs in her adult life. Some examples are nanny, waitress, receptionist, dispatcher, caterer, and finally teacher. She spent 10 years teaching 4th and 5th graders, until she finally felt the call to write. It's been plaguing her thoughts and dreams for years, and those thoughts finally fought their way out.

Jen loves to read, obsessively. She has an unhealthy attachment to her Kindle and is rarely seen without it. She'll read anything, but especially loves good smut or a post-apocalyptic young adult book.

After "retiring" from teaching, Jen sat down and wrote a book and then another and another and it was the most fun she's ever had working. She is self-published even though she's not sure how it works and hopes that people like her funny stories.

Jen is back in her native New Jersey and lives with her husband, daughter, and dog, enjoying suburban life.

 facebook.com/jenluerssen

twitter.com/authjenluerssen

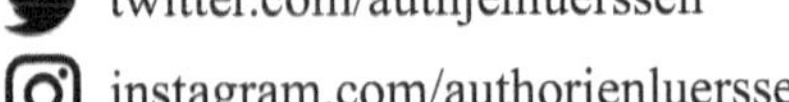 instagram.com/authorjenluerssen

Jen's books:

<u>Oopsie Series:</u>

Too Far to Care http://bit.ly/toofartocare

Grown Woman http://bit.ly/grownwomanoops

The International Language https://bit.ly/PaulDante

<u>LBI Romance:</u>

The Tide is High https://bit.ly/tideishighJL

<u>Novellas:</u>

High Note https://bit.ly/highnotenovella

Storm Brewing https://bit.ly/stormbrewing

<u>Smirk Series:</u>

F*cking Frank http://bit.ly/fckingfrank

Just Joe http://bit.ly/justjoesmirk

Salty Sebastian http://bit.ly/saltysebass